THE RED
BEACH HUT

Lynn Michell

First published by Inspired Quill: October 2017

Second edition published by Linen Press, London: January 2018

8 Maltings Lodge

Corney Reach Way

London

W4 2TT

www.linen-press.com

A CIP catalogue record for this book is available from the British Library.

Cover photograph: © Archangel
Cover design: Venetia Jackson / Zebedee Design

ISBN 9780993599750

Praise for The Red Beach Hut

'We live in polarised, paranoid times, suspicious about anything that departs from the norm. We are lucky to have writers like Lynn Michell to remind us that even here, even now, it is possible for the lonely and excluded to connect. It is rare to find such beauty and language as crisp and refreshing as the seaside it so powerfully evokes.'
– Maureen Freely, President of English PEN, novelist, translator and activist.

'From the first pages of this novel, Michell sets up an atmosphere of such convincing threat that the reader's expectations are on red alert.'
– Jenny Garrod. DURA. Dundee Univeriry Review of the Arts.

'Lynn Michell writes a beautifully innocent and endearing tale twisted by the tainted gaze of society's perverse darkness….She presents the reader with the delicate and fragile moments in which one reveals oneself to another and hopes that that this vulnerability will be met with compassion.'
– Isabelle Coy-Dibley for The Contemporary Small Press.

'A faded seaside town in Autumn is the perfect setting for this elegiac story of a vulnerable boy and the adult who befriends him…The sense of jeopardy is palpable. As the narrative flicks backwards and forwards, we're also reminded that in any part of Britain, ignorance and bigotry are never far away…I was left with the sensation of the fragility not just of seaside communities but of the knife-edge on which society is perched. A highly engag-ing and thought-provoking read.'
– Ali Bacon. *Between the Lines*

'The prose is achingly beautiful…I doubt there can be a better, more poetic or lyrical writer when it comes to sea and shore and to the timelessness of being out on the water in a boat…The boy Neville is exquisitely drawn, a wounded soul who counts stars and steps and grains of sand for security.'
– Avril Joy, Costa and People's Prize winning author

'A parable for our times…an intriguing book about secrets, assumptions, and consequences. I found it beautifully descriptive and the boy is beautifully realised.'
– Derek Thompson, Author of *StandPoint, Line of Sight, Cause & Effect, Shadow State.*

'A compelling book that examines bigotry, ignorance, redemption and friendship. Beautifully told too.'
– Heidi James, author of *Wounding.*

'Some of the best writing I've seen in a long time. The characterisation of Abbott and Neville is quite superb: the unease of the man and the perfectly credible affection he feels in response to the boy's humanity. The boy's moments of excitement, fear of happiness being snatched away and awareness of adult moods are all quite superbly drawn…Lynn Michell conjures up the somehow appealing desolation of a faded British seaside town. The opening paragraph is a tour de force. You want to jump right in.'

– Howard Sergeant, Writer and ghost writer.

'The innocence and trust of the relationship between Abbott and Neville is beautifully conceived.'

– Susie Nott-Bower. Author of *The Making of Her*.

'The magnificent part of The Red Beach Hut … is its touching on the ugliness and beauty of human nature – to be alone, an outsider and still seek out human connection…'

– SipnSee

'Delicately beautiful and gorgeously descriptive.'

– SarahLouise writes

'The writing in *The Red Beach Hut* is enthralling.'

– The Bibliophile Chronicles

'A convincing and compelling read. Neville's thoughts and speech effortlessly reflect that of a young child. An incredibly consistent character.'

– Lauren Parsons, Legend Press

'Beautifully written. The small English seaside town comes to life in front of your very eyes, and pretends to fall asleep while it keeps one eye open, watching the goings-on. '

– Bookmarked

'A brave and brilliant decision to have a child as one of the central protaganists…Neville is so beautifully drawn.'

– Ninja Book Box

'A rain-streaked, deserted British beach becomes a place of pilgrimage, of mystical retreat; an old beach hut offers warm sanctuary, revelation, truth-telling, consolation and love. It is fable for our time: a cautionary tale, shot through with light and loveliness.'

– Kate: Amazon reader

'Quietly and without dogma explores the consequences of the widespread intolerance in our society towards anyone who isn't vanilla flavoured.'

– Amazon reader:Bookworm

'Beautifully constructed, the narrative flows.'

– Amazon reader: Dr. Heinrich Uhlig

'A compelling book that examines bigotry, ignorance, redemption and friendship. Beautifully told too.'

– Amazon reader: Nomenclature

'The innocence and trust of the relationship between Abbott and Neville is beautifully conceived.'

– Susie Nott-Bower. Author of *The Making of Her.*

'The magnificent part of The Red Beach Hut … is its touching on the ugliness and beauty of human nature – to be alone, an outsider and still seek out human connection…'

– SipnSee

'Delicately beautiful and gorgeously descriptive.'

– SarahLouise writes

'The writing in *The Red Beach Hut* is enthralling.'

– The Bibliophile Chronicles

'A convincing and compelling read. Neville's thoughts and speech effortlessly reflect that of a young child. An incredibly consistent character.'

– Lauren Parsons, Legend Press

'Beautifully written. The small English seaside town comes to life in front of your very eyes, and pretends to fall asleep while it keeps one eye open, watching the goings-on. '

– Bookmarked

'A brave and brilliant decision to have a child as one of the central protaganists…Neville is so beautifully drawn.'

– Ninja Book Box

'A rain-streaked, deserted British beach becomes a place of pilgrimage, of mystical retreat; an old beach hut offers warm sanctuary, revelation, truth-telling, consolation and love. It is fable for our time: a cautionary tale, shot through with light and loveliness.'

– Kate: Amazon reader

'Quietly and without dogma explores the consequences of the widespread intolerance in our society towards anyone who isn't vanilla flavoured.'

– Amazon reader:Bookworm

'Beautifully constructed, the narrative flows.'

– Amazon reader: Dr. Heinrich Uhlig

'A compelling book that examines bigotry, ignorance, redemption and friendship. Beauti-fully told too.'

– Amazon reader: Nomenclature

1
Day 8

THE MAN AND BOY stood hand in hand on the top concrete step and stared, like they always did, towards the line where the sky melted into the sea. In the evening light it took a while for the air and water to fuse just as it took a few minutes for the two of them to feel at ease with each other. Then familiarity flooded back. With small nods the boy counted down to the amber-stained sand below. Seven. He took a breath, glanced up and waited.

'Ready?' Always the same word. The same starting gun. He liked that.

'Yup.'

'The sun's red,' the boy said.

'A blood orange.'

'A ball of fire.'

The effect was temporary Disneyland splashed on the

tired colours of the English coastal town. Normally on this shore, at this hour, there was only grey. Then a dimmer switch turned the shade in increments too small for the human eye to observe. Later, darkness would sweep in and the lights of bobbing, tethered boats would flicker on one by one to announce the night.

With the gentlest pressure from his hand to the smaller one, the man led the way, leaving behind the merry-go-round and whelk stalls and skittering sweet wrappers of the promenade. On the beach, tourists were folding their towels and rolling up their mats before heading for a pizza place that displayed plastic-coated photos of food, or a forlorn unlicensed cafe that served tea with a pre-heated meal. Afterwards those same people moved on to a themed bar or a disco that shrieked neon light and beamed ugly noise. None of that mattered. The backcloth of the town was not important to them.

'Why are we starting here instead of at your hut?' the boy asked, disturbed by the change in the routine. 'We always start at your hut. Same as yesterday and the day before. I like that.'

'I know you do. I'm sorry. I did tell you though. I don't want us to set off from the hut today.'

'Why?'

Although he had expected the question, the man took a while to reply. He wouldn't insult the boy with an easy verbal exit. As always, the boy waited patiently, trustingly, using the empty time to scan the watery landscape.

'I'm expecting visitors later this evening and I want to be there to meet them by myself.'

'Without me.'

'Well… yes. They don't know you.'

What I should be saying is that I'll be on my way very soon, but I'm not sure how to tell you that. I don't want to hurt you.

'So I can't come?'

Another long pause while he worked out an answer that was neither a lie nor the truth.

'It's a business meeting for grown-ups.'

'No kids?'

'Nope.'

'Can we start from your hut tomorrow?'

'Maybe.'

Damn.

He hated lying.

'I'd like to start from the hut. Same as always.' The boy glanced up, trying to catch and hold the man's gaze.

He's different today. Not just starting our walk from the promenade steps instead of his hut. He's quieter. Sadder. Not really paying attention to me. Like he's not really here. Like he's thinking about something else. I do that too sometimes.

It was the first time in their short week together that Abbott had been anything but open and direct and truthful with the boy. He'd made very sure he'd never taken advantage of him, never patronised him, never skidded away from the truth. Their relationship was built on honesty and the boy had responded day by day with a growing trust and ease.

'How about we walk barefoot today?' It was a ploy – to change the subject and to distract the child. But the boy was canny.

'Why?'

'Because... the sand is soft and powdery today after the rain and then the wind.'

'But we walk very close to the sea. The sand's damp there,' the boy said, puzzled and needing accuracy.

'That's true. Well... powdery until we reach the sea and then we can walk in the water and not worry about getting our shoes wet. That's good, isn't it?'

And I'm not going to get another chance for a long time to walk to the cove barefoot pretending to be a beach bum. There's no meeting for grown-ups or men from Mars. I'm leaving our beach very, very soon. I'm going away but I don't know how to tell you that. But if we leave our shoes here we have to come back here, so there's no possible excuse to stop at the hut where you'll see my bag ready and packed. All part of a cruelly necessary plan.

'OK.' Keen to please but also puzzled. Had he known the word, the boy would have said the vibes were different this evening. Jagged instead of calm. Edgy instead of reassuring.

'We can leave our shoes here. Hide them under the steps.'

'What if someone takes them?'

The man glanced down. Almost managed a smile. 'They won't,' he said. 'No danger of that.'

Without bending down to undo the laces, he trod out of his cheap, grubby trainers and kicked them out of sight under the last step. The boy sat down to undo the buckles of his flesh-coloured jelly sandals. He leant over to nudge them carefully into place, side by side but not quite touching, one inch away from the trainers. That done, he stood up and slipped his hand back into the man's and for a few moments gazed up with affection. The man smiled back, and felt like a complete heel.

You bastard.

Apart from today's different starting point, their walk was exactly the same as always. They set off in a straight line down to the sea's edge, then wheeled left and struck out along the curved shoreline towards the farthest point, where jagged rocks inhabited the sea, holding the fort and blocking the way to the smaller cove beyond.

As they walked, their bare feet left repeated signatures, large and small, in the sludgy tide-wet sand. Five and five, the boy counted silently. Ten and ten. Square heel and round toe marks frothed with toothpaste foam before the water took away the edges of the imprints. Looking back along the beach, he saw that the furthest dents were already erased, as if part of their walk together was vanishing. The tide was on the turn, sucking the shingle and rattling it backwards, reclaiming it for its own.

Despite the slight chill in the air, the man's hand was warm. He registered the boy's delicate pressure and the staccato squeezes of pleasure. The child's bones felt as fragile as a bird's but the man knew his spirit was strong.

'Yellow, lime green, white,' the boy chanted when they drew level with the row of sweetie-coloured beach huts, a long way back up the beach, lined up as straight as soldiers against the high concrete wall that was topped with a footpath for walkers too faint-hearted to venture this late along the beach.

'I don't like the white one.'

'I know.'

'I don't like the people in the white beach hut.'

'I know. We've talked about that a lot. Let's forget all about them. It's OK... they'll be gone soon. Summer's nearly finished.'

'Good. I don't want them here.'

They walked on.

'But they're there now,' the boy said, twisting his neck. 'They're staring at us. Like they always do.'

'Take no notice.'

'That's hard. I can feel them watching us.'

'They've got nothing better to do.'

'Oh... blue, another white one,' the boy continued, satisfied with the man's answer. 'Yours. Cherry red.'

'Pink. You missed one.' The man said on cue.

'I don't have to say pink. It's empty.'

'They're all empty.'

''Cept the white one,' he sighed. 'I mean all the other huts *had* people in, only they've gone away now but the pink one has had no-one in it all summer. It's empty.'

'OK. I understand.'

'Red *was* empty but not now because you live there. I like the red one best.'

The man allowed himself an ironic smile because this conversation, with a few variations, was as predictable as everything the boy did. Beyond the beach huts, there was only sand.

'OK…I want to know when. You say when.'

The man was expecting this too, would have been surprised if the words had not been spoken here, three-quarters of the way across the bay, where they could almost touch the closeness of night and true dark.

'*Why* can't I see it?' he persisted, despite several previous explanations.

'Because it happens slowly.' The man's voice was calm and patient, a baritone rumble above the rush and scatter of pebbles as the tide continued its task of pulling them back into the sea.

'But we can say *now* it's day and *now* it's night…'

'Only afterwards. There's light and dark but there's grey in between. Twilight. It doesn't matter if we aren't

7

sure. It's OK sometimes not to know. To be uncertain.'

'I like certain.'

'I know you do.'

'What about me and you? Are we *certain*?' He liked the word.

The man paused before answering. 'We are friends. That's certain. But I'm not here for more than a short stay. I told you that the first day we met. I said I'm here for a week or so. No longer.'

I won't even be here tonight. Nor tomorrow. The hut's tidied and I'm packed and ready to go the minute we part company this evening. While you're walking back to your house, I'll be on my way to the station.

'I wish it could be forever,' the boy said, choosing to ignore the man's nudge into a possibility of a parting he didn't want to acknowledge. 'We'll go for a walk together for a few more days yet though, won't we?'

'Well, I can't promise. I have to go back, you know.'

'Where to?'

'My house. Where I live.'

'You live in the red beach hut.'

'Only at the moment.'

This exchange had become a refrain.

'But you won't go yet.' It was a plea, not a statement.

The man let it lie.

'You *could* stay here even after summer ends,' the boy continued, against hope, but again he got no reply.

What he'd sensed earlier in the man – a nervous restlessness – grew stronger as they continued along the sand, and set off warning bells which made him feel unsure and fidgety. The arm linked to his own didn't swing along with the same pendulum bounce as they paced the beach, and the man sighed often. Instead of his lop-sided grin, his mouth was set in a line. His hand gripped harder. It was their habit to look out to sea, then at each other for an emotional weather check, but tonight the man was lifting his head and gazing round. As if he'd never seen the place before. As if he might be saying Goodbye to it. A tremor of anxiety ran down the boy's spine.

Abbott marched on knowing that his upset and guilt about leaving the place, transformed perhaps into something vague like restlessness, was being picked up by the boy who walked at his side. Like an emotional sniffer dog, he missed nothing. While not party to the plan ahead, nevertheless he was perfectly tuned in to the emotions that accompanied it.

I'll miss this place. And the boy.

'When will you take the boat out again?' the boy asked, glancing longingly back at the white dinghy tied up high on the shore close to the huts.

'Well, not today. The sea's rougher. Anyway, we did that yesterday. We can't go rowing every day.'

Excuses. Lies. The truth is that you've had your last trip in that dinghy.

'I loved it. It was the best thing I've ever done.' His eyes shone as he remembered his first ever sea journey, made of dreams and magic. Or like being in a movie, the way they'd slid across the bay with the man pulling steadily on the oars and the water lapping like a tune against the hull.

'Maybe tomorrow.'

'Maybe.'

In fact, never.

'Three hundred and ninety-seven,' the boy said. 'Seven too many.' But he was smiling, not anxious. As if admitting *counting is only a joke now.*

'No. We said ten more or ten less, remember, because sometimes we walk a bit faster or a bit slower so between three hundred and eighty-five and four hundred and five is fine.' The man continued the game. Playing serious.

'I know.' There was a faint hint of relief though the boy's counting didn't preoccupy him the way it had before he'd met the man. 'And two hundred and twenty-eight back to the hut.'

'Plus or minus five.'

'Do you remember… it was only two hundred and two the first time. You were walking so fast and I was trying to keep up!' He looked up and grinned. Gave a tug on the man's arm.

'I remember.'

'You didn't want me there, going for a walk with you the first time, did you?'

There was no point in lying. 'Well no, but things change.'

'Why not?'

'I wanted to be alone. I didn't know you. I thought you might be a pest.'

The boy smiled and leant in, ducking his curly head into the man's armpit, turning so that his free hand caught hold of the lapel of the old wool coat which was rough and scratchy, perhaps like the fur of a fox. It smelt of the sea. The man never teased him about his numbers.

At the farthest end, they stopped at the same exact spot, marked not by a stone or stick in the sand but by a line in the geography of the boy's mind. He could see the details of the landscape as sharply as if they were drawn in ink on paper: where the half-buried rocks were darker and more heavily indented and closely spaced; where the pools between them ran deeper with scrambling, sideways-scuttling crabs; where the black peaks rose from the sea in clusters of three and four and five with more sword edges and dagger points beneath the surface waiting to tear a swimmer's leg or tangle a fishing line or score a jagged scratch across a boat's hull.

Here, before the man came, at low tide he had often scrambled and slipped over the seaweed-slimed rocks to reach a cave that leaned out at the entrance to the next cove, a place of echoes and damp where he could stay for thirty minutes before the white water frills crept in to take possession and forced him to run back to safety. He could time thirty minutes exactly and get away safe every time.

Someone watching in the fast-fading light might have guessed that a father and son stood at the farthest end of the bay, huddled close, rock still, perhaps on holiday in this small dull coastal town, perhaps saying goodbye on their last night as darkness slowly blotted out even the sharpest of rocks and crags that stood so prominent, so unchangeably present in the clarity of day.

This was their check-point moment, where they acknowledged that they felt the same as the previous day and the day before that. The boy sensed the sea awash in the man's heart just like it occupied his own and that without it, perhaps, they would not have found one another. Turning to face the water, he thanked it for its gift. Then, at a nod from the man, the same as always, they wheeled round, turned their backs on the rock-strewn maelstrom and headed for the lights of the promenade. They would head further up the beach, walk on the softer sand close to the wall, climb back up the concrete steps and buy their cones of chips at the stall where the man gave them generous portions. Holding the vinegary packets against their bodies, they'd retreat the way they'd come and rush back to the intimacy of the red beach hut before the chips got cold.

They were halfway back to the steps when the man stiffened, transferring a warning shudder down his arm to the boy's hand. Neville had his head down, watching the crunch and spray of the drier sand as he placed each new footstep, heel then toes, exactly beside the man's larger ones. The sandpaper rasp made his soles tingle. He was counting when the man stopped, dropped the boy's hand and raised his own to his forehead, making a cap brim as if to shield his eyes from a bright sun, except that it was almost dark. When the boy raised his head and followed where the man stared, he could just make out a dark silhouette on the road above the huts and a bright spot of light that played all along the beach, back and forth, up and down, trying to pick out something or someone. At first the torch's light made wild sweeps all around them, missing their shadowy shapes in its random rovings. Then it found them and fixed on them, illuminating their faces and bodies. Again. Again. Back and forth. Abbott ducked and dodged but the light stuck to him. And to the boy.

'Darth Vader!' the boy said.

'Sshhh…'

A second shape appeared on the wall as if in answer to a shout or signal from the first. Two men stood in position, spaced out, stock still like soldiers on a watch tower. A second powerful torch came on and swept the shore until it too stopped on the two of them, blinding them.

Jim had said no reprisals. No witch hunt. What the

fuck's this then?

'Two Darth Vaders.'

'I said Be quiet.' Such harshness. And fear. The man who was always strong and steady sounded scared.

'Just people watching the boats...' the boy began, trying to reassure him, but worried because the man held his breath and rocked on the spot.

There was no mistaking they had come for him. The torch lights played up and down their bodies, marking them out as prey. But this was all wrong. It made no sense. Jim had turned up the previous evening to tell him that he was in the clear. There would be no dramatic reprisals. No-one would bother following him here and no-one would arrest him because what he had done was not serious. Stupid, regrettable, a dumb mistake, but not a criminal offence. He was a free man. Jim had said it was time to go back and face the music, but it wouldn't be the full orchestra. So what the hell was this? They *were* shining their torches on him. He wasn't imagining it. Perhaps this was a cock-up and he was caught up in someone else's drama. Or some event in the town that had triggered a search party down here.

No, Abbott. It's you they want.

'Listen,' Abbott said to the boy, his voice tight. 'You're to run home. Leave me here and run.' His words came in breathless bursts. Like gunfire. 'Run back towards the promenade. In this light, they might not see you. They've seen me but I'm big and tall. Perhaps not you.'

Some hope in those flood lights. But there's a small chance he can slip away.

'You want to run?' The boy asked, perhaps deliberately mistaking the words. This wasn't the game they played on their way back to the red beach hut. If anything they slowed down, anticipating the pleasure to come. Yet even as he asked, he knew this wasn't a game.

'For God's sake, Neville, just do as I say. Leave me and run. You're not part of this. I don't want you to be part of this.'

'Part of what?'

Right now, I don't know. I haven't a clue. Unless Jim was lying and they've come for me after all...but he would never lie. He'd tracked me down and travelled all the way here to tell me I was in the clear, for god's sake. You might get a phone call and a knuckle-rapping, he'd said. Not two men in heavy duty with search lights.

He racked his brain. The only mistake he could think of was that he'd taken the boy out in the dinghy. OK, that was a bit daft. Someone might have seen them and put a scary gloss on it. He'd gone for a row with a child in the bay without asking a parent's permission but anyone watching would have seen them arrive safely back at the shore with no harm done. The child had been a bit late home but there was nothing new in that. Abbot had spent the rest of the evening talking to Jim. They'd parted on good terms with Abbott's promise that he'd come out of hiding and return. Tonight. After he'd gone for one last walk with the boy.

There are a hundred scenarios to explain this but none of them make a damned bit of sense. Why would anyone want to corner me on this dreary wasteland of a beach?

The boy stared through the darkness, drinking in the drama, still too astonished to be frightened. One of the robots broke ranks and ran along the promenade and down the steps to the beach. Still a long way off. The other one jumped down to the roof of one of the huts and was scrambling, clinging then falling to the deck below. Voices carried across the air above the gentle evening shush of the sea. Two dark outlines appeared on the beach like weighty ghosts heading toward them. Hard, heavy running that must have left boot-shaped pits in the wet sand because these people were not bare-foot and were in a terrible hurry.

'Run, for christ's sake!'

'Why?'

'Don't ask. Just run away as fast as you can. OK?'

'Where?'

'I told you.' The man's voice was harsh. 'Go up the beach. Hide between the huts like you did before. Anywhere…but leave me. Go!' The man gave the boy a push.

But the boy leaned harder against the man and held fast to a fist full of his coat, choosing to wait with him. He saw stamping, panting, shouting people draw near enough for him to see not robots but humans with black hoody things with eye-holes pulled down over their faces. The first man was closing in on them fast. Maybe soldiers. Maybe police.

Neville started counting. *Two*, he said to himself. *No…there's another further away. Three.* He shut his mouth, then opened it again. 'There's my mum!' he shouted. 'My mum's running too, but she's a long way behind.'

She'll be so mad at me. She doesn't know about the man or the red beach hut. And I don't know why these men are running hard at us with bright lights. I'll stay close to Abbott. Whatever happens, I want to stay here with him. He's my friend.

2
Day 2

'HURRY UP, SON… sandals on!'

Neville looked up. His mum was painting her mouth lollypop pink with one hand without looking in the mirror and with the other was smoothing a large red satin square over her bed. The shiny sheet was thrown on every evening followed by the pink cushions that she kept in the cupboard. One was heart-shaped. All this she did in her five o'clock costume.

She looks like an acrobat in a circus. Or a tight rope walker, except they have bare feet and she'll put on her silver shoes with high heels. You can't get across a rope in high heels.

He watched her sigh through the familiar preparations in her tight leggings and tiny sequin top. Her face was an apricot colour, not bare, freckled skin like usual. And sooty eyes with the big black eyelashes she stuck on with a squeeze of glue.

A pretty clown. Maybe she does tricks like those women in the circus she'd taken him to. Tricks and acrobatics. She can't swing from a trapeze though. Or fly through the air. Or jump through hoops that flare with orange fire. Not much room to do anything in this flat.

Her high heels were ready by the bed. Now she was poking silver hoop earrings through the holes in her ears.

'Sorry. Wrong order.' Neville sighed. 'I did the right one first.'

'OK, do them again in the right order. But hurry up! I have to start work soon.'

'There's no-one here yet.'

'Any minute.'

'A man?'

'Yup. Same as always.'

'Which one?'

'For heavens' sake, son! You don't know any of them. They're just men who come and spend some time with me. Then they pay me.'

'Which man today?'

'It doesn't matter.'

But it does. Once a man was unkind to you. Once a man shouted at you and made you cry. I heard through the wall because I was at home sick that day. I heard. Afterwards he came into my room and said things. I don't want that man to come back.

'Not the man who shouted...'

Oh no. I've let the words slip out because I was thinking about it. Sometimes it's hard to know when I'm talking to myself inside my head and when I'm talking out loud. The man came into my room afterwards while she was in her room and said, Don't you dare say a word or bad things will happen. To her and to you. He smelt bad.

'What are you talking about? What man?'

'Nothing.'

'It can't be nothing. What's worrying you, son?'

'The man who shouted.'

What's all this about out of the blue? Yeah, blokes yell at me all the time, and worse, but it goes with the game. Shame the kid happened to be at home that day. I got the tosser out fast enough. Not one of my regulars. An unpleasant bugger. Plastered.

'We've talked about it, son. I told you that man won't come back. It won't happen again.' Under the flatness of her voice he heard a tiny tremble. He heard a whisper of fear. She was breathing faster.

'I don't know that 'cause I'm not here. I'm far away on the beach. I was here that day 'cause I wasn't well and couldn't go for my walk.'

'I know, son, I know. I'm very, very sorry that happened. It was bad luck you were here that evening.'

'OK.' He felt no reassurance.

'Look, we'll talk about it again if you want. Later.'

He blinked back tears that threatened to spill but managed to plough on with the questions which filled up the place where the hurt was lodged.

'What do you do with the men?'

She sighed loudly. 'You've asked me that so many times and I've told you so many times. I don't do much. Keep them company and chat to them. Cheer them up a bit and send them away happy. OK?'

'Why do you dress up first?'

She heard the delaying tactic. ''Cause they like women in fancy clothes. A bit different from normal. Bit of fun, like.'

He bent over his sandals again, his forehead as creased as a paper fan. 'I'm ready.'

She came to him, bent and kissed his cheek. 'You don't mind, do you, going to the beach and playing by yourself for a while?' She looked into his grey eyes until he answered.

'Nope.' It was honest.

'It's not for long, is it? Just 'til the clock on the pier says six-thirty. OK?'

'OK.'

'It's a nice evening. It will still be light by the time you come home. You can look in the pools. Count the crabs.' She knew she was inventing pleasures and making excuses but what other option was there? Best to put a cheerful gloss on what had to be.

'Yup.'

She bent down again and hugged him. 'You know I'd like to come with you but some evenings I can't. I'm sorry, son.'

'I already said. I don't mind. I like the beach. I like the sea. I like to count things.'

Sharon knew the counting had become worse again recently. It had faded for a long time and he'd seemed more secure, especially while Janie was working here with her, but now she sensed he was hiding his feelings beneath the numbers again. It troubled her. 'You can tell me what you counted when you come back. Here's a pound for a cone of chips.'

'OK.' He shoved it deep in his pocket.

Left pocket. Twelve chips in a cone. Sometimes thirteen or fourteen. Seventeen once when the man poked a few extra ones in and winked at him. The man was always nice to him.

'And remember…don't talk to strangers.' It was flung out. A parting shot.

'You said.'

'I know but it's important so I'm just reminding you.'

'Is the old lady in the deck chair with the tartan rug over her knees a stranger? She always says Hello and sometimes she gives me a sweet in a crinkly wrapper.'

Heavens! Why on earth did I start up on this?

'Um… no… because you see her every day. You know her.'

'I don't *know* her. She just says Hello. What about the ice-cream man?'

'No, of course not. He's been here as along as we have.'

'Four years.'

'Yeah… so we know him. We see him all the time.'

'What about the man and woman in the white hut? I don't like them. They won't talk to me. The man told me to go away. He wasn't kind.'

'Take no notice, son. I don't think they like children. They're not nice and they're not friendly but they're certainly not strangers. They live in the town and have been sitting in that hut of theirs for years.'

Spying on other people. Reported me to the police for working from home with Janie so now we can't look out for each other. Two's a brothel. One's acceptable even if she gets beaten up. I expect the white hut pair would like that. Pair of meddling sodding self-righteous buggers.

'So who's a stranger?'

'Someone you don't know at all…never seen before… someone who comes up to you and starts up a conversation or asks you to get into a car…look we'll talk about it later. When you come back. We'll talk about everything that's bothering you. Now go! Scoot! Love you!'

He stood, flesh-coloured jelly sandals buckled in the correct order, green anorak zipped almost to his chin, and with a backward look, made his way, counting, down the three steps of the ground floor flat in the concrete block where they lived, one street back from the beach. On their narrow balcony they could see the sea shimmering in tiny teasing patches between roofs and walls and roads. They could see small postcards of sand and deck chairs and holiday makers but not the whole picture. Neville walked past more flats like theirs with small iron balconies that gave the same glimpses of the sea. At the end of the road, before heading down the pedestrian street to the promenade, he turned and waved. His mother waved back then shut the door as a car drove too quickly round the corner and pulled up outside the block.

VW Golf. Red. Alloy wheels. FA59STR. Says FASTER. Yup, fourth time. Not that man though. Not the one who shouted. Good.

A man got out, walked up the steps and rang the bell. He wasn't wearing a circus outfit.

It was true that he really didn't mind his solitary outings. Alone, he could stare at things from different angles and think about them for a long time without being interrupted. Without grown-ups asking stupid questions. At school there was too much noise and too many people who talked all the time and pushed and shoved so that he had no space and his breathing grew tight. The teachers made him do things he didn't want to do. In the playground, bigger boys teased him and laughed at him. They pushed him about. He had to remember not to count things out loud.

This late afternoon time was his very own time.

3
Day 3

COUNTING HIS FOOTSTEPS under his breath, he reached the promenade and checked that the little girl with the brown plaits was going up and down, up and down on the blue and purple horse with gold paint peeling off its mane. Each time the carousel reached the spot where her mother stood watching, the girl lifted one hand from the painted mane and waved. In the jazz-coloured cars that were way too small for them, the two big boys with shaved heads and earrings were half-leaning and half-falling out, standing up and hanging on with one hand and shouting too loudly. Sometimes rude words. It was all just the same. The same as every day. Good.

Down the broad concrete steps, dirty and dusted with sand from feet that had walked up and down the whole long day. He trod carefully, not wanting gritty grains rubbing the soles of his feet in his jelly sandals, translucent, not red or green so he could see his toes and count them if he felt unsettled and needed to do one to ten. Both ways. Of course he *knew*. It was just nice to know the answer was always the same. Especially if worrying thoughts hung in his head and wouldn't go away.

The flat stretch of sand was messed and scuffed with footprints from the running and playing and settling and squirming to sunbathe. He searched for the few clean untrodden places and aimed for a landing on their newness. Big steps. Sideways steps. Jumping steps. He made his way down to the sea, close enough to watch its frilly edge but not close enough to get his sandals wet. A white whirl of a shell caught his eye. A Spindle Shell, not a Common Whelk, with only the tiniest chip on its lip so good enough to go in his pocket. He liked the unhurt ones.

On the flat field of sand, some people were packing up for the day, scraping sand off their sticky bodies, rubbing the soles of their feet, and stuffing damp bathing things into limp Tesco bags. Others lingered, flat like cut-out people, shiny pink in the setting sun. He knew they would suck up the last rays before giving up and going away. By the time he had walked to the rocks at the very far end, the beach would be almost empty and the lights on the promenade stalls would start to flicker on. Fish and chips – his stall. Hamburgers. Whelks. Hot dogs. Ice-cream. Candy Floss.

Like yesterday and every other day, he set off along the beach, past the row of huts, taking care not to go too close because the couple who didn't like him were out on their verandah, staring. They made him nervous, so he called Hello and they shouted back angrily. *Go away!* He didn't hear the rest because he turned his head and hummed loudly. Stupid! His mum had told him to ignore them.

He bent his head forward and counted his footsteps to the point where the sand grew coarse and changed to shingle that felt bumpy and sharp beneath the soles of his jelly sandals. At the very end of the curved bay, a stack of sharp-tipped black rocks jutted up in groups of four and five and six. Like sentinels marching backwards into the sea. Water burst and broke over them, blocking his way to the next smaller cove. Only at very low tide, when the pools ran quietly, was he daring enough to walk through and around them on puddled sand while he held his breath and counted his steps because it was dangerous. In the next cove was a gaping, echoing cave whose roof leaned out like a canopy towards the sea. He'd been inside and shouted and heard his voice bounce back to him. If the sea ran inside too soon, he'd be trapped.

Today, like every day, he stood whisper-still and waited. Today, like every day, he scanned the wet rock tips, then dipped his eyes downwards into the busy, tight-swirling pools – water prisoners that couldn't roll away – his heart pounding in anticipation of a glimpse of the forever elusive shimmer of blue-green scales, a whale-like tail, a pale eye, seaweed hair. A slippery seal movement over the rocks.

Nope. Not today. Can't see one. Maybe tomorrow.

Giving up, he turned and made his way back along the shore, darker now with only a few people left behind who looked like shadows.

Halfway back, he stopped and lined himself up, feet together facing the water, opposite the sailing boat with the green hull that rose and fell on its chain and sea-sawed in the choppy waves. *Sprite 5191.* It had a top structure that probably led into a cabin with a bunk bed, but although he stopped here every evening, Neville had never seen anyone on it. A lonely boat that never went anywhere.

It was while nodding his head in tune with the boat's rocking motion and counting the jerking ups and downs that he noticed the man. A few yards beyond his own watching point, another person watched too, standing still and staring out to sea. The same as him. Most people on the beach came in two and threes or in whole noisy running-around, ball-kicking groups, but Neville knew that this man was attached to nobody. He had no anchor and no chain. The man was like a parcel tied up with invisible brown paper and string so no-one could look inside. He held himself tight and together inside the thick knee-length coat and the cap pulled low on his head. Neville stared at him, looking left, his attention pulled away from the rhythm of the boat, and at the very same moment the man turned his head to the right. Their eyes met and locked in a brief but definite glance of greeting and acknowledgement. Pulling his hand from his pocket, Neville waved. Once. The man nodded, waved back, then turned on his heel and walked further along the beach to the rocks. After checking and re-checking that the man didn't look back, Neville continued on his way, turning round every few steps to follow the man's back. He needed to know.

If you slipped in by the last hut, hard against the wall, you could vanish into its dark shadow. No-one could see you. And Neville knew that the pink hut had been empty all summer and so no-one was inside to catch him hiding there. He edged in, flattened himself to a cardboard cut-out, and waited.

His breath held in anticipation. He was as invisible as a ghost. He already knew where the man would end his walk because tonight the tide was high so there was no way through to the cove. He gave him an exact five minutes to stare at the rocks, counting them away, then imagined him turning on his heel and setting off again. Twenty-one, twenty two, twenty-three – yup, there he was, walking back really fast, his arms swinging. When he was fifty yards away, Neville pressed his skinny body harder against the wall but kept counting and popped his head out at the exact moment when the man was climbing the steps to the small verandah outside the red hut. He saw him reach out with a key and turn it in the lock. Only when he heard the door click shut again did he emerge and watch from a few feet away. Across the window, black curtain shapes were pulled together. Then something darker was drawn down from top to bottom. Soon a faint orange light showed round the edges and leaked out into the evening, dim at first but growing brighter and stronger. He imagined the inside of the hut softly lit. Red. Warm. Safe.

It's ages and ages since the old woman was here. She was nice. Kind. She gave me biscuits and drinks. We went for walks together and collected shells. We sat on the verandah and watched the boats. I miss her. Now someone else has come to live in the red beach hut.

When Neville set off again, he lifted his shoulders in little shrugs of excitement because something different and new had happened. Not scary new but nice new.

I shan't tell anyone. Not even my mum. Maybe I'm the only one who knows and it's a secret. Tomorrow I'll come back and see if the man is still here. Maybe he'll talk to me.

Back on the promenade, he walked with bouncy steps to the chip stall and reached up on tip-toe to give the man inside his pound coin.

'Hello there! You look cheerful today. The usual?' the man asked, though they both knew the answer.

'Yup.'

The man turned and dug his little shovel into the stack of chips before draining them on a perforated metal tray. Neville watched to see how full he filled the paper cone. Same as always.

'There you go. You tuck into those.' The man smiled. 'All alone again?'

'Yup.'

Why does the man always ask the same question? He knows I'm always alone. But he doesn't know something different happened today.

Neville turned to go, holding the secret inside.

'Enjoy your chips, son. See you tomorrow.'

Behind the stall, sitting on the wall, he swung his legs and slowly poked the blunt finger-shapes into his mouth. Lick. Chew. Swallow. Greasy and mouth-puckering. Sour with vinegar and gritty with salt.

And in his mind he made up a story about the man who had come to live in the red beach hut.

4
Day 5

'IMPOSSIBLE,' HE HAD said out loud, his head bent over his small grubby hand which, rounded with inward-curled fingers, was doing a stalwart but hopeless job of containing a fistful of sand. More escaped than stayed put, in thin-running streams. 'Completely impossible.' He sounded beaten. The words sighed from the depths of his being.

He'd set up camp on the sand in front of the three steps up to the red hut, but so absorbed had be become in his self-imposed task that he didn't hear the click of a door being quietly closed, nor did he look up when the just perceptible shadow of a tall figure fell over his hunched form. The man heard the childish sigh of exasperation.

That boy from the other night who waved. Don't reply. Ignore him. Walk straight past him. Get rid of him and tell him not to come here again.

'What's impossible?' The words were out before he had time to catch them. A reflex from his very recent past when he never failed to answer a young person's question.

The boy looked up. 'Counting grains of sand,' he said. 'You see…I don't know what's a real grain and what's a bit of shell or a bit of dirt. So how can I count them? And they're so tiny they keep sliding off my hand.' Defeated, he lifted his head again and stared into the deep-set brown eyes of the man who stood next to him. Someone older might have interpreted that look as a fusion of wry amusement and fretful annoyance but the boy was too engrossed in his task and too young to make any such interpretation.

'Do *you* know?'

The memory of the previous evening's chance encounter with its afterglow of red light on grey sand had drawn Neville back to the same spot. Counting the sand, though, had its origins much further back. It was something he'd been thinking about for ages as he'd walked along the beach on his solitary five o'clock excursions. Of course it would be impossible to get an exact number. That was absurd. Anyone knew that. But if he could count a handful, it would be a start, and then he could crawl the width of the beach on his hands and knees to find out how many hand widths fitted between the huts and the sea. Then multiply the two numbers and he'd have an *estimate* of a very thin slice of the beach. *Estimate* was a favourite new word because it offered a useful let-out when you knew you couldn't be perfectly, absolutely correct and exact.

He'd come to the hut hoping that the man would come out for a walk, as he had the previous day. Always patient, Neville had sat himself down to wait, but time passed slowly and the door didn't open so he'd scooped up a handful of powdery sand and started to count, at first with excitement but then with increasing frustration and despondency as his goal literally slipped away and he had to start over again. And again. After a while he forgot all about the man.

'I don't know either,' the man said brusquely, stopping only for a second before preparing to continue on his way. He would turn his back on the child. He'd discourage him from ever coming here again.

'Why?'

He sought a sharp retort but failed to find one. 'No-one knows. Anyway it doesn't matter.'

'It *does* matter.' The boy sighed and opened his two sand-crusted palms in a gesture of hopelessness.

Abbott should have left it at that. But it was too soon and too close to what he had left. He responded as he had to every cornered boy, every difficult boy, every brutalised boy, every boy with a criminal record who, perhaps after weeks or months, finally said something. Asked a question. Opened a tiny window onto his ragged and wounded soul.

And so he failed to seize the second opportunity in two minutes to bring the whole ridiculous conversation to a close. A full stop. He could easily have said something dismissively cross. Others would have done. Or something bland which would have told the boy he didn't give a damn about his bloody sand. He could have brushed past him in silence and marched purposefully along the beach. He could have told him to go away and not come back. That he was trespassing on private property. That he was being a nuisance. But the troubled grey eyes stopped him.

Walk! he told himself. *For Christ's sake, Abbott, let it go! Let him go. You're not a child-mender anymore.*

Instead, he folded his tall body to fit beside the child who had moved up a notch to the lowest step. When he looked into the boy's face he observed and judged that the child was vulnerable, sensitive, observant and wise beyond his years. Reading boys' faces had been his trade for a very long time and he was good at it. In a heartbeat, Abbott was jettisoned back into one of those anonymous, grimly furnished rooms in which a truculent young person sat on the other side of a scabbed table, big trainers sticking out on the Lino floor while *he* searched for a small crack in a long-formed, anger-hardened shell of defence. To offer a response to a troubled child was a habit too deeply ingrained for him to ignore. He gave. He helped. He listened. He held out a hand. He was known among his colleagues to be one of the best.

'It doesn't matter,' he told the boy.

'It does.'

'No, it doesn't because the thing is…we can never know. There are way too many grains of sand to count and thinking about it makes our heads hurt. So we have to let it go. Let the sand be.'

'So we'll never know?'

'No. There are thousands and millions of grains of sand but the secret of the number belongs to the sand, not us.'

Tiny tell-tale creases on his brow and twitches of his mouth told Abbott the boy was thinking very hard.

'The sand has a secret,' he said finally. 'And it can't ever tell us.'

'Exactly. The sand was here long before we were.'

'How long?'

'Oh for thousands of years. The cliffs and rocks have been bashed and broken into tiny fragments almost forever. The waves have ground them to smithereens.'

'I know. That's why I can't count them.' He was smiling now.

'So we can leave the secret with the sand. We don't need to know the answer because the sand was here long before we were.'

'The sand's secret number.' The boy nodded, satisfied and relieved. This he understood.

'Like the sea.' Despite himself, Abbott was warming to the subject. 'We'll never know how many drops of water there are in that bay. Too many drops for us humans to think about.'

Clear grey eyes, wide open and as round as an owl's, soaked up the information.

'So let's leave the sand and the sea to themselves, shall we? To exist.'

'To *exist*?'

'To be themselves.'

'OK.'

'They are very, very big and that's all we need to know.'

The boy nodded again. The man's comforting words explained things he hadn't worked out for himself. No-one had ever talked to him this way. Usually grown-ups treated him like a much younger child. Or they gave him quick, stupid answers they hadn't thought about and he knew were wrong.

'Wow!' he said. 'That's so right. I'm glad the sand and the sea have secret numbers.'

For a while they sat in silence.

Abbott put down a hand to lever himself up and to end the conversation. To end the encounter. He had done his duty and could walk on and leave the boy to his own company. But the boy anticipated the movement away – from him and from further conversation – and jumped in with another question that needed an answer. In fact, there were an infinite number of questions he wanted to ask on the subject of numbers but most grown-ups refused to answer.

'But we do need to know *some* numbers?'

The delaying tactic was obvious and blatant and they both knew it but it was another good question. Abbott sighed and recognised with one quick glance a curious child whose thirst for knowledge was not quenched.

'Yes, of course we need to know the number of some things.'

'Like what? What number do you need to know?' The voice was expectant.

'Well… for me it's important to know how many tea bags are left in the box. I would hate to get back from my walk and not be able to make a cup of tea.'

The boy giggled. Silly answer, but sensible too.

'What about numbers we *like* to know?' he asked after another long, considered pause. 'Not *need* but *like*. There are lots of numbers I'd like to know.'

Abbott was sinking up to his neck but even while squirming, the recently dumped persona continued to respond with a quiet honesty.

'OK. It's different for everybody but I like to know… to check… how many stars make up Orion.'

'I know Orion. The star man with the sword.'

'That's the one. Well, that constellation follows me around wherever I go. When I left home it was above my house. Here, it's up there in the sky above the hut and it makes me smile that it's still there.'

'Why?'

'Because it's reassuring. Like my very own night lights. I look up…and there they are.'

Abbott felt the boy's tremble of pleasure and understanding.

'I like knowing that it has ten stars,' Abbott continued. 'It's constant. Do you know that word?'

'No'

'It means the same. Never changing.'

'Oh. *Constant.*' The boy repeated the new word with its lovely sound and meaning. 'Exactly, exactly the same.'

'That's right.'

'Do you live in the red hut now?' He had to know.

Over the following days Abbott would often hear these abrupt changes of topic as if the boy's thoughts turned on a coin. He acknowledged the grass-hopper mind of a young lad but also the smart tactic of jumping sideways to the core of things, to something he desperately wanted to know. What to reply now? Abbott knew the boy would be able to detect a lie.

'Yes, I'm staying here for a few days.'

'I know that already actually. I know who comes to all the huts 'cause I'm here every day. But everyone has left now. Too cold.'

'Well, summer's almost over.'

'But the two people I don't like still come most days. They live in the town and go home every night.'

Abbott smiled at the flood of information.

'You don't go home, do you?' the boy asked.

'No.'

'Why?'

The man waited a beat.

Jesus. How had this happened?

'I want to live by the sea for a bit. I like staying in the beach hut. I'm having a bit of a holiday.'

'But the holidays have finished. Nearly.'

'I like being here now. I haven't come to sunbathe.'

'What, then?'

You fell straight into that one.

'For a break. A rest.'

'OK. But the huts are for day time.'

'Not always. They're big enough to live in. For a while.'

'Do you have a bed?'

'Yes.'

'And a kitchen?'

For fuck's sake! He nodded.

'And a TV?'

'No TV.'

'Why?'

'No electricity. And I'd rather watch the sea.'

The boy put his head on one side, considering. 'Me too.'

There was a pause, which again Abbott would come to recognise and acknowledge. The boy was good at silence.

Then, 'Can I see inside?'

This time the answer was instant and very definite. 'No.'

'Another day?'

'No.'

The boy's face closed and tightened but Abbott ignored it. He had no intention of ever letting him inside. He had every intention of shedding the child after today's impromptu but lingering encounter. He'd make sure they never bumped into each other again, even if it meant peering out of the window and scouring the sands before exiting the hut. He'd stay inside if he saw the lad anywhere in sight. He'd soon get tired of hanging around in vain. And if there *was* a next time, there'd be no conversation. He would not provide any answers. The last thing Abbott needed right now was a loose cannon of a child.

He pulled himself upright.

'Well… nice to meet you… and it's been an interesting chat but I'm going for a walk now. You go on home.'

The single leap down all three steps was meant to signal a definite ending. On the sand, he set his face towards the cove and shoved his hands in his pockets.

'It's not time to go home yet.'

Abbott said nothing. Didn't look back at the child.

'Can I come with you?' The small voice trailed after him.

'No. I want to walk by myself. Very fast. I don't want company. I want to be alone. You go on your way now.'

'Maybe I'll see you another day.' The hope was hesitantly spoken by a child used to being rebuffed.

'Maybe.'

A lie. An idiot lie. And cruel. Why offer him a tiny ray of hope when you know he'll curl his hand around it and hang on to it like those bloody unreliable and elusive grains of sand?

Abbott set off with resolute strides, angry with himself and fretting over his fall into familiarity with a boy with whom he absolutely didn't want any involvement.

If he had turned his head, which he deliberately didn't do, he would have seen that he was being followed at a distance by a small downcast figure who kicked sorrowfully at the sand with every footstep. The boy hung well back and made no attempt to catch up with the man, understanding and allowing him his privacy because he knew not to bother him, not at that special place, perhaps not ever again. He stopped well short of the cove and sat down on the sand, near other huddles of people so he was kind of hidden. People didn't want to be bothered with him. But not to look up proved impossible and his repeated glances towards the cove brought the reward he wanted. After twenty minutes, here was the man, as predicted, on his way back. After he had passed, Neville got to his feet and tried to turn himself into a shadow. He weaved in and out of the people on the beach, head down, body hunched. The man paced on, resolutely ignoring his follower and cursed himself again for allowing his carefully constructed defence barriers of privacy to be breached by a child's question.

How could it be otherwise? Three days ago he'd had his arms wrapped round a swearing, struggling, red-faced thirteen year old who was trying to head butt him and kick him in the shins in a hopeless attempt to do a runner. The child had been running his whole life, just one in a long line of boys whom Abbott took on and tried to push off the fast track to a life behind bars or the filth and cardboard of the homeless, or a lonely dirty death from a needle in a vein. Abbott had seen it all. The boys who ended up in the Young Offender Unit had come from poverty and despair, from neglect and indifference, from cruelty and abuse. Instead of school, their patch was a street corner. Instead of teachers, they answered to drug dealers and pimps. Some were as young as ten or eleven with eyes that spoke of a premature emotional death.

So to have ignored a lonely boy counting sand would have been to go against the grain of what he did intuitively, with patience and with skill. Most days he sat down with a boy condemned as a write-off. A boy who was already damaged goods. This lad was much younger than most of those in the unit but Abbott saw the first signs of the same vulnerability, like he was standing precariously on one side of a set of scales that could tilt either way.

Nah, that's rubbish, Abbott. You know nothing about the kid. You're pulling facts out of thin air. Don't give him another thought. He's just a boy on a beach. Chances are you'll never see him again.

Back at the door of his hut, stamping the sand off his trainers and already with a hand on the door knob, he made his last stupid mistake. He turned. And looked straight at a boy whose shoulder-drooped pose spoke of disappointment and rejection. Across the sand whose grains could not be counted, their eyes met again.

Fuck!

5
Day 4

'**M**UM?'
    'Yes, son...' Sharon was in fast forward. It was that time of day again. Neville watched her slam plates and cups into the dishwasher and drag a sponge over the kitchen work surface. Between grabbing objects and returning them to shelves and cupboards, and plumping cushions on the brown velour sofa, she took urgent gulps from a tumbler of red wine and dragged on a crumply cigarette she'd rolled herself. It smelt different from the ones from the packets. He glanced at the clock but knew it was twenty minutes before she started work. Until he had to leave the house and walk on the beach. This was the time of day when she was wound up too tight and too busy to pay him attention and didn't want his questions but he had to ask.

    'Mum, you know those beach huts...'

'Yeah.' On automatic pilot. 'Just hang on, son, till I've got the place sorted.'

The living room will do. Don't know why I bother. They never notice, for fuck's sake. There's only one room that interests them. Only one place in the damn room. The rest of the flat could be a pig sty for all they care. The floor would do for most of them.

It was always the same frantic late afternoon routine after she'd met Neville from school, walked him home, given him his tea and cleared up while keeping an eye on the clock and knowing she had less than half an hour before her clients started to arrive. It never got any easier. She dragged the cork out of another bottle of cheap Tesco red, dumped a third into a large glass and drank it down like water. Breathing exasperated, angry sighs coloured with the tea-leaf smoke, she moved across the hall into the bedroom. Neville followed.

Why does she always leave everything to the last minute? Why does she do this work that makes her cross and upset?

'Why don't you find a different job?' He'd asked her so many times, wanting her to be happier, until she'd told him to stop asking. Now it slipped out again.

'I've told you. There are none.'

'Must be one.'

'Son, in this dump...dead and deserted for more than half the year...there are no jobs that will pay the rent and feed us. Believe me, I've looked.'

'How about working in a cafe? That'd be nice and warm.'

'They're closed except in summer.'

'You could work in summer then.'

'And earn enough to keep us all year? Don't be daft.'

'That big warehouse place?'

'Nope.' Then mumbled to herself, 'Yeah. Great idea, son. Zero hour contracts... half a living wage...no security... no pension... bloody Tory government.'

'What?'

'Doesn't matter. Grown up talk. I was just saying the jobs are all rubbish.'

'Nothing else then?'

'Nothing.'

'Sorry, mum.' He *was* sorry she had to do work she didn't like. The five o'clock work.

'Not your fault, son.' She bent and kissed the top of his head. 'If I seem cross, it's nothing to do with you. You're a good boy and I love you and I'm proud of you. You help me a lot by going for a walk every day. You don't complain even on days when it's raining.' She sighed and blinked back tears. She asked a lot of him.

'I don't mind the rain. I sit in the bus shelter and eat my chips and look at the numbers of the buses. I know them all and the times they come.'

'I know. You're such a good kid. We'll manage.' Her head on one side, she stared at him for a long time with troubled eyes.

'Mum, you know the beach huts…' The question wouldn't stay inside.

'Yes…' She paused for another long suck on the cigarette and looked his way.

'What's inside them?'

'Nothing much. Deck chairs and towels and stuff for the beach.'

'I can't see inside them when I walk past.'

'There's nothing much to see. Just huts. Like big garden sheds.'

'Most of them are locked up now. People have stopped coming to sit outside them.'

'Yeah.' She was only half-listening as she opened drawers and pulled out her thin sparkly costume and silver leggings.

'There's still people in the white one. When it's sunny there's deck chairs on the verandah. Two people, quite old. They drink mugs of coffee and read the paper.' This wasn't the point but he hesitated, not wanting to say the wrong thing now when she was already in a bad mood. Then he blurted it out. 'They're not nice. They don't like me. I said Hello once and they told me to go away.' He frowned.

'Yeah, you said. Don't worry about it.'

'Why don't they say Hello to me?'

'Some people don't like kids.'

He pulled a face like he definitely knew that. 'And the other huts?'

'Oh heavens, I don't know. I expect they belong to townies who come for a holiday and use the huts during the day.'

'Why?'

She took a drag and blew the smoke out slowly. 'Because it's nice to have somewhere to put all your beach stuff and nice to sit and watch the sea. Even on a cold day, you can sit inside with the door open and have a warm drink. Better than three quid for a lousy coffee on the promenade.'

'Do you buy the huts?'

'Heavens, so many questions today. Yeah, I think so. They cost a fortune, son.'

'Just for a hut. Why?'

'I suppose they're fashionable or something. Very sought after.'

'People don't live in them though, do they?' He held his breath. It was the question he'd left 'til last in case she got suspicious.

'No, son. I've said. They're just huts for days on the beach.'

'Are you sure no-one lives in any of the huts?'

'Quite sure…why are you asking me all this?'

'Just wondering.'

'OK, let me get on now. No more questions.'

Lost in thought, he walked to the window and whispered the line of crayon colours under his breath, starting with yellow and ending with pink, while Sharon dragged her duvet off the bed and stuffed it into a space at the bottom of her wardrobe. The shiny satin sheet came flowing off the top shelf to replace the simple, flowered patterned cover. Neville knew there were two silky red covers. One on the bed and one in the wash. The pillows joined the daytime duvet and were replaced by the pink cushions. His mum unfolded her sequin circus costume and started to tug off her tight jeans. Her forehead was crumpled and her mouth a hard line.

'But *could* you live in one?'

'In one *what*?'

'*Beach hut* of course. I already said.'

Sharon blew out a heavy sigh that ruffled her blonde fringe. 'No. Not really. It would be very cramped. Why? Do you want us to move into one?'

Neville giggled. 'No. But someone might live in one.'

'For heaven's sake, son! People *don't* so this is a silly conversation and this isn't a good time to pester me. You know that. Enough! Better start to get ready for your walk. Find your jelly shoes.'

'Sandals.'

'Whatever.'

'They're always by the door.'

'Then put them on! And your anorak. And leave me in peace to get ready.'

She was wrong. Someone *did* live in one of the huts.

Neville hugged himself at the thought that it might be a secret that only he knew. He remembered exactly what they had talked about – the sand's secret number and the tea-bags and Orion. The word *constant*.

The next day he had played hide and seek – well mostly just hide – to see if it was true and the man *was* staying there. As soon as he'd reached the beach, he'd raced right along the back, close to the wall and had taken up sentry duty behind the end hut, the pink one, next to the red one. And held his breath and waited. He'd heard the noise of the door being pushed open first. Then the man's footsteps. Neville caught a glimpse of him standing on the verandah looking up and down the shore, his head turned one way then the other. Like he was checking something before setting off with long strides along the beach towards the cove. Neville popped in and out like a jack-in-a-box, finding the tall figure again and again as he marched along the beach and then vanished round the corner close to the cove and stayed there for ages and ages. But Neville had stayed, even though it was dark and he was cold. He stayed long enough to see the man walk back, a shadow on a shadowy beach, see him unlock the door of the red beach hut and go inside. The light came on slowly until it was bright enough to beam out over the verandah for a few minutes. A hand-shape pulled the red curtains together and tugged down the blind. The light was warm and soft, like the man had lit Christmas candles.

He'd stayed so long tucked against the wall that his hands went numb and there'd been no time for chips and the pound coin had stayed in his right pocket. He'd been late home, the darkness thick and complete.

Now, on his door step, he wriggled with pride and pleasure while he buckled his left jelly sandal, because he hadn't told anyone what he knew, not even his mum.

6
Day 1

T HEIR DOUBLE CONSOLE was parked in the back corner of the Young Offender Unit's second floor, separate from but facing the sprawling rectangle of linked cubicles that took up the whole of the open-plan room. In the other back corner stood the coffee machine and water cooler. When the walls had come down, and the separate offices had been demolished, the two friends had grabbed the desks at the back, citing age and experience and 'Don't mess with us', and no-one had argued. They were liked and respected. They'd both served a lot of time, this side of the bars. On the floor below were the seminar and counselling rooms, while IT and Admin took up the ground floor in a warren of as yet unconverted offices.

Abbott strode in, stepped over to his desk, flung down a brown paper bag containing his lunch and threw himself into the chair. A glance at Jim and the fingers moving in *furioso* mode told him not to interrupt. An empty noodles carton and plastic coffee cup signified *his* lunch had already ended. Abbott's own desk was littered with invoices and receipts; a small paper mountain close to sliding over the edge of the desk. He pulled his Tesco sandwich from its bag, tore open the wrapper and casually scanned his screen, looking for where he had left off. The sandwich halted half-way to his mouth. He looked harder. Put it down on the pile of papers. He hunched and bent forward, closer to the screen. He stared some more. Pressed a few keys. Pressed more. His body stiffened.

'What!' His forehead creased into a frown as he tapped on keys, more furiously this time. 'Now what's going on? I didn't leave it like this!'

He knew he was talking to himself. Jim carried on typing in his semi-detached cubicle, headphones on, two fingers of each hand doggedly banging on the keys. Without aural feedback, his typing had gradually increased in volume until it was intrusively loud. Sometimes Abbott resorted to earplugs or slammed on his own headphones to cut out the energetic clatter. It had become a joke around the room – Jim sounding like he was working on a very old Olivetti. Others would look up, shake their heads and mime sticking fingers in their ears.

'This isn't right,' Abbott mumbled, scratching his head. 'My spreadsheet's all scrambled.'

He hit Back, tried to get up previous versions, clicked

on History. The keys seemed to be jammed. Then, as he watched, numbers began to fall out of the table to the bottom of the screen where they landed in an untidy pile. Alphabetti Spaghetti only numbers not letters.

'Fuck's sake!' he said, louder this time. 'Bloody hell…I've never seen anything like it! The thing's taken on a life of its own.' He slammed his hands flat on his desk. 'Jim!'

'What?' Jim asked without taking his attention away from his own screen.

'My computer's going insane here. Look…kamikaze numbers leaping out of the spreadsheet and throwing themselves to certain death at the bottom of the screen. Look at them! I'd just about finished my monthly expenses. Typed them all into an Excel sheet. Took me all morning. I go out to Tesco for a sandwich and when I come back it's not here…well it's here but it's like some kids' cartoon. Animated numbers. Look at this garbage.'

'Don't ask me, mate. Computers operate themselves.' Jim continued typing.

'Jim.' It was a question. Abbott had dropped the humour. His mouth was dry.

'Aw c'mon, Abbott. You don't need me to hold your hand. Click Back. Click History. If you saved it, it'll still be there.'

'Of course I bloody saved it.' Abbott raised his voice. 'I'd typed in about a thousand little numbers for petrol and lousy sandwiches and I wasn't planning on doing it all again....'

'I know. Did mine yesterday.'

Abbott hung his head. A flush spread from his forehead down his cheeks to his neck as he saw and began to understand. When once more he tried to get rid of the crumbling spreadsheet, his hands shook so hard he couldn't hit the right keys and sweat beaded his forehead.

'Jim! Will you stop typing, turn your head this way and look at my screen. Something's really wrong here, mate.'

Jim removed the headphones and swivelled in his chair to face his colleague over the low wood partition.

'Christ!'

'Exactly.'

'It's emptying itself.'

'Like when you press rewind on a video. I typed the numbers in and now they're removing themselves. Can't remember the order but maybe in reverse to me entering them.'

'That *is* weird!'

'Thank you.'

The two of them watched in silence. Then Jim got up and came round to Abbott's side.

'Budge,' he said, but Abbott had already got up to give him his seat. He leaned over his friend as Jim put his fingers on the keyboard. And typed very loudly. He tried the usual combos. Swore. Tried to pull down menus. The numbers kept falling.

'It's jammed.'

'Tell me about it.'

'Better turn it off.'

'Right.'

Jim pressed OFF. The screen blackened.

'Give it a few minutes to come to its senses. Never seen anything like that before. You may have to call IT to get it sorted.'

'I don't have time for this, Jim.'

'Me neither. Do we ever?'

Jim pressed ON. The machine hummed back to life. The icons popped back up. The menus and side bars reappeared. Closed windows reopened. For a few moments it looked promising. Normal even. The spreadsheet appeared for a split second but then vanished to leave a totally blank screen showing a tiny envelope whose flap opened and shut, opened and shut.

'What's that?'

'No idea. Broken. Rubbish. Call IT.' Jim was already turning away.

'Hang on, Jim. Better open that envelope.' Abbott's voice was edgy.

'Nah. Leave it alone. Get on the buzzer to IT.'

'See if you can open it first.'

Jim shook his head but turned back to the machine. Behind the envelope, the blank screen slowly came to life like the opening shots of an avant-garde film. Nothing sharp, nothing very clear, as if someone was operating a brightness switch, making viewers wait. Too dark and blurred to make out at first, as it came into focus there was no mistaking what it showed. A slow-motion parade of men in pornographic poses progressed left to right before falling out of the bottom right corner. Jim's hands froze above the keys. He shook his head in disbelief.

'Open the envelope, Jim. Quick. Before it vanishes.'

'It's opening itself. Jesus.' It took a lot to make a dent in Jim's carapace but he was clearly shaken. 'The cursor's moving by itself. I'm not doing a thing…'

Jim and Abbott watched. A note jumped out of the envelope and unfolded itself.

The Guard Dogs have been here.

No Poof Is Safe

Woof Woof!!!

'Fucking hackers!' Jim sighed. 'Look, it's either total bad luck or… maybe somebody who doesn't like…'

'Gays.'

'Yeah. Though I wouldn't jump to that conclusion.'

Abbott read the message. Twice. Three times. His face turned ashen. Sweat broke out on his neck and trickled behind his collar. Jim didn't move. Disbelief and disgust silenced the pair of them.

'You have to report this. Now.'

Abbott hesitated. Jim noticed. Noticed too the beads of sweat and trembling hands.

'Why are you looking at me like that? You don't have

to deal with this on your own.'

'Let me think about it first, Jim.' Abbott's voice was hard as rock.

'What the fuck for?' Exasperation cut across his sympathy for his friend. OK, he knew from the rare bits of personal information Abbott shared that he still got insults for being gay but this was something else altogether.

Abbott took a deep breath and looked at his friend. His words sounded raw and wounded. 'It might not be that clear cut.'

'What do you mean? Your machine's been hacked. Either the hacker has thrown a wild card that's landed face up or it's a hate crime aimed at you, Abbott. And others like you. Could be either. Get IT to take your computer away and dig inside it to see if they can get a trace on this. Hand this garbage to someone higher up the food chain and get on with your work. Forget it. It's rubbish.'

But Abbott sat motionless, his head in his hands. Jim got up and paced the small space behind their desks. He felt his friend's pain but it was out of character for him to react this badly. Abbott was made of stern stuff. His private life rarely intruded.

'OK, let me tell you something. It's more bad news but not this kind of shit. Give you something else to think about. Want to hear?'

'Whatever?' A lifeless word without interest or concern.

'Look, I've spent the morning typing up a report on

one of ours which has to be with the boss an hour ago.'

Silence.

'Been trying to put a positive spin on things. The boy's reoffended and if I don't make a good case for him he goes down and we've wasted a year working with him.'

'Who?'

'Zac.'

Abbott rallied as if a switch had been thrown. The real man stepped into the place where a fearful ghost had taken up residence. 'Oh no.'

'Yup'

'I thought we had him sorted. What's he done?'

'Only beat up someone in a pub so bad he's in hospital. Police want him charged for GBH and put away this time. No more chances. *No more bloody therapy.*'

'He's seventeen. I've spent hours with that lad. He's bright. He's capable. He was listening. I thought.'

'So? He blew. One down, a few hundred to go.'

'Shit.' However many times it happened, it was still a blow. A defeat. For a few minutes Abbott recalled the face of a troubled boy who was almost at the finishing post. 'I'm sorry,' he said, before collapsing in on himself again. He glanced up at the screen.

'Look, turn the damn thing off and call IT,' Jim said, angry now. With the hacker and with Abbott. They'd all wasted enough time. He was back inside his own console, lifting his hands to return to the report when Abbott lifted his eyes and looked straight at him. Jim saw fear, like an animal caught in a car's headlamps. But Abbott didn't *do* fear. Abbott was bomb proof.

'What?' Jim asked. 'Is there something you're not telling me?'

Silence. Abbott glanced across, making Jim afraid.

'You're making very heavy weather of this,' he said, dead serious. 'I mean, it's clear what's happened, mate. This is nasty but you're getting it a bit out of proportion. I mean you've done nothing to deserve it.' He tried to hide the hesitation.

'No.' After a split second.

'It's not personal. This hacker has nothing on you.'

Abbott didn't reply.

'I asked a question.'

'He does.'

'What?'

'He knows I'm gay.'

'You can't assume that. He may have left the same nastiness on a dozen computers.' Again Jim floundered. Something unsaid hung in the air like the static before a storm. He'd worked with Abbott long enough to know that the man was troubled beyond the fact of being hacked. He'd seen his colleague take worse taunts in his stride when someone stepped out of line. For some reason this went deeper.

'Want to tell me?'

'Maybe it *is* personal, Jim.' The words emerged through anxiety as sharp as pain.

'You mean you know who did it?'

'No. Maybe.'

'Which means what, exactly? That you have something to hide? Look, I'm sorry to ask...'

'I don't know, Jim. Someone I....Once before...' Sentences emerged half-finished and frayed at the ends until Abbott gave up, folded his arms over the papers and the egg sandwich and laid his head on his desk.

'If there's previous, you'd better tell me.' Jim said quietly. 'I'll help.'

'Maybe beyond help.' Quiet, despairing words.

Jim got up, went to the coffee machine and returned with two full, flimsy plastic cups.

'Here.'

'Thanks.' Abbott lifted his head and looked straight into Jim's eyes. Then bent to sip the nasty scalding liquid.

In the six years they'd worked together, Jim had never seen his mate crushed like this. The man's shoulders were broader than most.

'It *is* because of your private life you're so worried, isn't it?' There was a reluctance in Jim's question because work was work and mostly they left out the rest.

Abbott said nothing.

'OK, let's take the worst-case scenario. You've been singled out. Personally I think it's highly unlikely but if it is, I'm sorry you're having to take it. There's still a lot of hatred aimed at people.... like you.' He tried for tact but knew he was spouting truisms.

'*You're* telling *me* that?'

Jim sighed. 'Look, don't wrong foot me, mate...I'm just saying either it's random or, unlikely, he knows you're gay. Out comes the poisonous drivel. He's probably targeted others.'

'Or just me.'

Jim heard, and looked round the room before continuing. It was almost empty apart from a few guys typing at their stations down the other end. It was OK to talk.

'You've no reason to think that.' Jim said quietly. 'Shit like this happens all the time. OK. Look, I'm not prying into your private life. If you want to tell me, I'm happy to listen. I might be able to stop you worrying. If there's something in your past...well maybe I can put your mind at rest. I mean...most of us know you're gay.' His voice trailed off.

'I've never hidden it.'

'But right now you're worried the hacker has dumped his filth on you for a reason? It's not random?'

What haven't you told me, Abbott?

Jim looked across. The uneaten sandwich leaked grease into the pile of papers while Abbott shredded the brown paper bag into smaller and smaller fragments, covering his desk and the floor with brown confetti. Was Abbott being paranoid?

Jim scratched his head. He too looked pale and subdued. 'I'll do whatever I can. I bet if we ask the Tekkies to do some probing we'll find this has gone to others besides you.'

Silence.

'OK, mate. I have to finish this report but if you want to go for a pint after work…'

'Thanks, Jim.'

It was in a leaden silence that the two recommenced work, one truly worried about his friend, one in too much emotional turmoil to make sense of anything that he should or had to do that day. His heart thumped so hard he imagined it visible through his shirt. The internal tape loop played louder and louder and on it was the story he hadn't told Jim. The one about Luke. The one that would clinch his dismissal.

'I'm going home,' Abbott said at four o'clock. 'Can't concentrate.'

'Right.'

Abbott started stuffing files into his shoulder bag.

'You need to call IT before you go,' Jim reminded him.

'I'll do it tomorrow.'

'No, you need to do it now. You're not thinking straight. If someone has hacked into your computer, they may have accessed secure files. Confidential police records.'

'I told you…it's nothing to do with work. They're not after criminal records.'

'We don't know that.'

Silence.

'Look, do you want *me* to report it. Get IT up here?'

'I'd much rather not.'

'Right.' And stupidly, Jim let it go. Because his friend looked near to breaking point.

He decided against shooting his usual pathetic parting joke about being good or not doing anything he wouldn't do. The emotional ground had shifted between them and was no longer solid.

7
Day 2

A BBOTT WAS NOT at his desk the next day. Jim was told there'd been a phone call citing flu but the blatant lie hovered like an accusation until Jim picked up the phone and told the boss what had happened. The response was fairly neutral at first, even sympathetic as he listened to the description of the images on the screen and the contents of the envelope, but when Jim admitted that his colleague hadn't called IT nor reported the hacking immediately, a tight-lipped displeasure poured through the earpiece of the phone. To be expected. They would both be summoned. Jim was implicit too. For being a witness and not reporting any of it either. Mouth clamped shut, Jim listened, not daring to interrupt, to the torrent of verbiage about stuff he already knew. Yup, a weak link in the chain is a danger to the whole team and the entire organisation. Yup, you have to report something that's maybe suspicious and wrong even if it means ratting on your colleague. Yup, it's that kind of thing that gives them all the security and confidence to do what they have to do. Yup, if someone managed to hack into Abbott's computer, it's possible he *also* managed to gain access to the Police National Computer and criminal records. Yup, Jim agrees he must partly shoulder the blame and deserves to take the rap too. He knew as well as Abbott what he had to do.

'But your colleague will fall harder,' the voice said coldly. 'Unless he comes back here fast with a good explanation for why he said nothing.' Then the official gale blew itself out because the next statement was spoken with a trace of sadness. 'Abbott's one of the best. I'd hate to see him go.'

Jim sat for a long time with his head in his hands. Yes, the storm clouds would blow over but he and Abbott would still have to stand out in the rain for a long time until tempers calmed and they were seen to be shamed and contrite.

He picked up the phone and pressed speed dial.

'Abbott?'

Long moments of breathing before, 'What?'

'You've got to come in and report what happened. The two of us.'

More breathing. 'Yeah.' Meaning No.

'I've told the chief.'

'And…' Jim heard the word spoken through gritted

72

teeth.

'He's not well pleased.'

'Jim, I've worked for twelve years without putting a foot wrong…'

'Exactly. You're respected. Top notch. So you're not going to be kicked out for one lapse. Look, the boss wasn't happy but he'll relent. His first reaction was bound to be knee-jerk hard. Things'll calm down.'

'And it won't make any difference.'

'Listen, Abbott. After the shouting, he said you're good.'

Silence.

'Did you hear?'

Abbott didn't answer straight away. 'I did something unforgivable.'

'That's a bit out of proportion. I think you're over-reacting…'

'Perhaps.'

'For fuck's sake, Abbott! You failed to report something suspicious on your computer. You aren't the first and you won't be the last. You didn't steal anything or corrupt somebody or take advantage…'

'I can do without the lecture.'

'Yeah but you just went home. You haven't checked your personal files. You need to. All of them. Bank accounts, pay slips…'

'You don't understand, Jim.'

'I think I do understand, Abbott. I was here. IT will

check if the hacker reached further inside to information that's not personal.'

Abbott interrupted again. 'They won't have.'

'What gives you this god-like insight, Abbott?'

'A hunch.'

'Oh great. In our line of work, a hunch is the best way to go.' Jim was pissed off.

The silence was opaque. Even over the line Jim tuned in to a breath-held tension.

'Am I missing something here?'

Nothing.

'I mean, you seem more exercised about a homophobic note than about a possible breach of inflammable information…' Jim waited, worried now.

Finally Abbott spoke. 'Jim, go and get yourself yelled at and get back to work. You were only the sidekick. No-one's going to throw the book at you. Won't be pleasant, but you'll survive.'

'I'm not worried about me. Yeah, I'll survive. It's you.'

'Forget about me.'

'What?'

'I said forget about me. I'm not coming back.'

Jim raked his fingers through his buzz-cut hair and shook his head in disbelief. He'd worked with Abbott for six years. They were a good team. This was so wide of the mark it was crazy. The guy was grounded, wise and capable. As the boss had said, one of the best.

'Can you tell me what's going on?' he asked gently.

'Because there's another layer here you're not telling me about. Yeah?'

'No.'

'No layer or no you won't….'

'No, I won't tell you. Fuck's sake, let it go.'

Never had Jim heard his friend so troubled. Or so scared. 'Something outside this incident?' He counted until Abbott spoke again. Waiting for the outburst. But it didn't come.

'Once…' His voice broke.

'Once what?' Jim asked quietly, pushing back his panic.

'I made a mistake once before, Jim.'

'Christ. What kind of a mistake? At work?'

'No. Personal. One mistake… but they'll make the link…'

'How long ago?'

'Five years.'

'Aw come on, man. That's history.' Jim sounded as unconvinced as he felt. His heart was racing.

'Interpol's good at history.' Abbott said quietly.

'Right.'

Silence.

'What did you do? Christ, sorry to even ask…'

'It's OK.' Abbott interrupted. 'You need to know. It was one bloody stupid night …too much booze…the guy was after more excitement than I could offer him and wanted me to see some erotica…asked for my card.'

'Why yours?'

'He'd been for a long swim in a rough sea. No wallet. No card.'

'I thought no-one used cards after the banks agreed to cooperate in tracking down porn merchants…'

'Yeah. That came in ten years ago. Buyers switched to alternative currencies like Bitcoin…'

'So why did he use your credit card, for fucks' sake?'

'He was careless… irresponsible. He was like that, a law unto himself. I took my eye off the ball. My fault.'

'What did he want you to see?' Jim had trouble forming the next words. 'Kiddie porn?'

'No! Christ, no! Pretty adolescent boys…'

'How old?'

'Fifteen…sixteen…I didn't look…shut it down.'

'Under age?'

'Under age.'

'And then what?'

'I lost it. I chucked him out. Told him to stay away from me.'

'He went?'

'Yeah…after an almighty row. It got physical.'

Jim thought it through. 'Could be worse.'

Abbott heard the unasked questions and relented because his mate had been tactful enough not to ask.

'It was while I was off sick. Well, not sick…in need of a rest. I went to a retreat.'

'I remember. We'd not been working together long.'

'I met someone there. A free spirit. We had one wild night and he fucked me up.'

In more ways than one.

Jim breathed out. Even smiled. 'Then forget it, Abbott. The chances are they'll never look. Their minds are on a breach of security.'

'They're good. They're smart. They smell rats and find them.'

'They won't be bothered.'

'Don't you believe it. Not with all the stuff in the papers. Smoking out gays is a national pastime.'

'Where's the laptop you used? I mean five years ago?'

'I destroyed the hard disc and chucked the rest in the sea.'

Stupid bloody question, Jim! We've seen others do the same enough times.

'Abbott, honestly, you don't have to panic, mate. Look, I'm going to say this once more, slowly and simply. Yesterday someone hacked into your machine, showed you a load of rotten apples and left hate mail. Our friends in HQ are on red alert in case he did more but my guess is this attack is homophobic. Your computer's clean apart from one break in and your only crime is not reporting it. No-one's thinking beyond that scenario. What you've just told me has no part in this. End of story.'

'That's the benign interpretation.'

'That's the likely and probable and *obvious* interpretation, but if you stay away, the antennae will start to waver.'

'The antennae are *already* waving. You don't see them. Yeah, on the surface we're all totally PC about gays, but there are some who don't like us working with youngsters. They keep their mouths shut but I hear them. It's something you learn to do. And there's hysteria out there as they hunt down the next Jimmy Savile or Rolf Harris. Pedophilia is the bad flavour of the month. Of the year. Couldn't be a worse time. The media circus is prancing around with their tongues hanging out and I could be the next fall guy.'

'Hang on! You're not making sense. The media is after the celebs and the household names. Nasty big thrashing fish. They're not interested in you, mate. You're a minnow. Sorry to describe you as a small fish.'

'I work with lads, Jim. They prefer their youth workers straight. I'm a sitting target.'

'Forget it. OK, you're gay. Not the only one here. You guys seem to be drawn to this kind of work, and are good at it.'

'Maybe we can relate to the lads.'

'Exactly. And you don't put your gender preferences on display.'

'It's called non-scene. A gay man who keeps his sex life very private.'

Jim acknowledged the truth with his silence. 'Abbott, listen! You're one of the best men we have. The lads trust you. Come back. This is rubbish, mate. Total fucking rubbish.'

'Yeah, I was good at my job. But I'm finished.'

'You're being paranoid. You're making it up as you go along. You've invented a link between a slip five years ago and a hacker who hates homos. Have you been in touch with this guy since?'

'No. Never heard from him.'

'So why...look it's five years ago, Abbott. Five years.'

'People have long memories.'

'The sooner you come back the quicker it'll be sorted. Staying away makes things look worse.'

'Can't face it, Jim. It'll be a witch hunt.'

'Not true. That's not true, Abbott! Come back and we'll sort it together. You're making a mountain—'

But Abbott had put the phone down.

For a while, Abbott stood still, replaying the conversation, but it only firmed up his decision. No way would he stay around to be hounded out of his workplace and displayed in six-foot high letters all over the red tops. GAY MAN WORKS AND PLAYS WITH BOYS. They'd just love a story exposing him as another pervert working with vulnerable boys and young men. He'd rather do a runner than have the wrong label slapped on his forehead. He'd rather die than be falsely named and shamed, perhaps dragging with him work mates who were solid.

The decision was made. In the bedroom of his small

modern flat, he dragged a large dusty hold-all and his back pack from the top of the wardrobe. His hands shook as he pulled old jeans and a couple of old shirts off their hangers and stuffed them in. He would need very little. From his chest of drawers he grabbed t-shirts, socks, underwear. A pair of flip-flops. A Swiss army knife. His torch. Toothbrush, tooth paste and razor from the bathroom shelf. He slid down a couple of clean towels and some bedding from the shelf in the airing cupboard.

There'll be stuff there.

He emptied the meagre offerings of the kitchen cupboards and the contents of the fridge into a heavy duty black plastic sack which he tied and took outside to dump in the communal bin in the road. Back, breathless, he unplugged his lap-top and connector and snapped them into the work issue bag he used to carry it to and from work, then into the inner pocket he slid his passport and driving licence. Finally notepads, pens, pencils, charger.

For Christ sake, I can buy stuff there, he told himself. *I'm going to an English sea-side resort not a yoga centre in an Indian jungle.*

Planning was impossible. In his adrenalin-charged state rational thought evaporated and his head spun as if he'd drunk several triple espressos. This calm, steady, quiet man was in emotional overdrive. A switch had been flicked and the fear and panic that he'd kept lidded for five years exploded into possibility. Probability. Irrational but all-encompassing panic flooded his body.

When he's finished packing, he tidied the flat, made his bed, cleaned the kitchen, put out more rubbish, and hoovered the carpet. He lived simply, an almost monk-like existence, saving his energy for his work, so preparations for an exit were quickly done. Then he sat at his desk and removed every letter, every utility bill, every birthday card, every note and reminder to himself, every single piece of paper, and stuffed the lot into a metal box he used for his few household tools. There must be no trace.

On his small balcony at the back, he put a match to his past and present, careful to smother the smoke as best he could. It was a jerry built block of sixties flats inhabited by busy, single folk who, like him, worked long hours.

Like a murderer, he thought, *removing evidence and wiping fingerprints from the scene of the crime. Except I'm erasing myself.*

And he knew full well that however much paper he burned, electronic records listing every single fact about him remained untouched so it was all pointless nonsense. He was not burning evidence but energy, a pulsing tide that swept through his veins and crashed around his head like wild waves. This slash and burn was only a way of killing time and occupying his shaking hands while he waited, because it was still too early to make his move. His plan was to arrive at the coast in the early hours of the morning when the place would be deserted. The last train left at eleven fifteen and would get him there soon after one. He had hours to wait. Agonising hours.

He deliberately skirted the framed photograph that had been in his desk drawer wrapped in tissue paper. He unwrapped it and wrapped it up again. He picked it up and put it down, packed it and unpacked it, even once throwing it into the metal bin while flames and specks of soot shot upwards. But he pulled it out again. Part of the simple frame and one of his fingers were singed. Unable to make up his mind, he slammed it down on his desk where it could wait until the moment he went through the door. As he sat and shuffled his feet and watched the clock, there it stayed, the only personal item left in the flat, face down. And then he could bear it no longer. He leapt out of his chair and lifted it by one corner, like handling a live lobster with waving pincers, and scrutinised the features captured in that moment when the button was pressed. Emotions raced and collided – joy, pain, guilt, regret, anger – while he opened his bag and slid it between the folded shirts.

He shouldn't have looked. The features came to life. The mouth opened and spoke in that burr of a northern accent that had been as alluring as the strong unusual face and the youthful body.

'Put the fucking camera down and come back inside, sweetheart. I've just swum a mile in that wicked sea and my shoulders need rubbing. Other parts of me too. It's our last

day. I'm going to miss you.'

'Yeah, Luke,' Abbott said out loud. 'Unfortunately I've had to think a lot about you in the last two days. How you screwed me in so many ways. How the sky just fell in and I'm thinking you had a hand in it. Did you hack into my machine? Are you still mad at me for sending you packing?' Voiced out loud, it sounded ridiculous and incredible. Abbott even smiled. 'No. It'd be too much trouble. And anyway, why? You had others waiting in the queue.'

What happened that night was insanity. I blame the place. The end-of-the-world isolation. I blame your bloody beautiful face.

But that was the end of the story.

8
Days ago

I T HAD BEEN five years since Abbott had broken his own and the institution's rules by allowing himself to get too involved in a case. Yeah, he knew exactly how to handle each turbulent, stroppy, disturbed, closed-off boy who came to him to be turned around, if only by a few degrees. Yeah, he remembered the lectures during training about staying an emotional arm's length away from everyone he dealt with and about leaving the angst and anger behind in the interview room. A man working with disturbed boys couldn't move in too close or the relationship would not work. Yeah, he was good at his job and could handle the fall out when things back-fired and a kid screwed up despite his input and efforts.

Once, and once only in a long career, he got it badly wrong.

He'd been assigned to a kid nick-named DJ, a musically talented, angry boy of fifteen who illegally played various clubs and circuits for money for his habit, claiming to be eighteen. Already cautioned for shop-lifting and dealing, this time he'd been hauled in for GBH. His victim, his face rearranged by a broken bottle and his ribs staved in, had lived, but the boy's bitter fury at the world burned on. He was coiled and ready to attack again. Didn't matter who.

Nothing new here, Abbott had thought on meeting the lad for the first time. The usual background of poverty, alcohol and drugs. Like many others, this kid stood little chance of emerging intact when his childhood had been a brew of abuse and brutality.

But the extra ingredient in the otherwise volatile mix was DJ's musicality.

Get through to him that way, Abbott decided early on. *He speaks that language, not words.*

An electronic keyboard became the third presence in the sessions and for weeks it stood on a table, resolutely ignored. Just as Abbott's quiet, patient questioning and attempts at conversation were ignored. His head always down, DJ drummed broken tunes and rhythms with his fingers on the table and hummed out loud over everything Abbott said. And then, after hours and days and weeks, came the monosyllabic answers. Fleeting eye contact. Then words and sentences. One day he got up, sauntered to the keyboard and played *Stairway To Heaven*. Into the melody he poured so much pain and poignancy that Abbott had to blink away tears.

From that day, between short staccato bursts of talking, he ran for the safety of the keyboard and closed his mouth on further verbal interference. Drip by drip, Abbott squeezed out his story: a childhood of violence and physical harm from a male member of the family. When he spoke about his step-father, DJ gritted his teeth and spat words. He hated all men. His anger burned. But when he played, his carapace cracked open and Abbott tip-toed inside. There, curled in a foetal position, he saw a soul so sensitive, so musically precocious, that he was frightened to disturb it for fear of it breaking. When one evening DJ played something he'd written on the keyboard, Abbott's neck dimpled with goose bumps. The boy had a rare talent that didn't dare show its face and around it he had built a prison fence topped with razor wire. No wonder he was fucked up.

They talked about music and ways of working with music. Abbott scoured the net for keyboard courses for lads like this one. He dropped the suggestion quietly on the table, letting it rest there. The response came a few weeks later in the form of the tiniest flicker of hope in DJ's eyes. He spent more time with this lad than any other, pushing down others on his waiting list or handing them to colleagues so he could continue working with him. It became a personal mission, and it should never have been that, to rescue him and to send him to a place where the curled foetus dared to be born. Abbott crossed the line labeled professional objectivity and became involved.

Jim was fairly new to the job while all this was going on, but one day he took his hands from his computer, leaned across the wooden partition and said, 'You're not going to want to hear what I have to say, mate, but I've been given the job of breaking bad news.'

'What?' Abbott was busy typing.

'How about we get ourselves some of that piss-water and have a seat in the conference room over there? It's vacant.'

'Tell me here.'

'Rather not.'

'What's this about?'

'Come on, mate.' Jim got up and went to the drinks machine, returned with two flimsy, dripping beakers and headed for the empty room. He shut the door behind Abbott and motioned him to sit down.

'I'd rather stand. Who's run amok this time?'

'DJ.'

A stone fell into his stomach. 'What's he done?'

'Half-killed a guy who was apparently playing the piano all wrong in a club. DJ had done his session and was high as a kite. He shouted to the guy several times to stop fucking up the tunes, then put a knife in his spine when the pianist declined. The guy's in Stoke Mandeville. If he does play the piano again it will be in a wheel-chair.'

'Christ.' Abbott sank into the chair and put his head in his hands. Beads of sweat coated his face and hands. 'And?'

'DJ's been moved to the secure unit. No more nice counselling sessions for him. We've lost him.'

'Why wasn't I told before?'

'The top boys asked me to break the news. They know how much time and effort you've invested. We all know how close you got.'

As if someone had thrown him a dead weight, Abbott immediately shouldered the blame. He'd used music to peel open a tin can of emotions that perhaps should have remained sealed. For a few days he staggered around, operating on brain stem, but the weight of his guilt and responsibility grew heavier and heavier until he ground to a halt. One morning Jim found him at his desk with his head on his folded arms. He'd seen it happen to others but Abbott was stronger than most and no-one expected this reaction.

'You need time out, mate.'

Abbott turned his head sideways. His eyes were bloodshot from lack of sleep and his indulgence in the numbing powers of alcohol. 'Can't. Too much to do. Five new cases this morning.'

'Exactly. But you can't function like this and you can't help them. You need a break.'

'Nah…just a bad day.'

'Several bad days.'

'This isn't my usual style.' A hint of the old irony. He wasn't completely lost.

'I know. We *all* know that. You're usually bomb proof. But this job can get to the best of us. You just had a tough one.'

'Yeah…maybe I could do with a day off.' Never did Abbott think he would hear himself say those words.

'You're to take a week off.'

'Who says?'

'Me. I ratted on you but I was worried. Anyway I'm not the only one who's been watching. Words have been exchanged. The boss has told me to tell you to take a few days off. He's waiting to tell you himself.'

'What?' Abbott sat bolt upright, still fighting the knowledge that others knew. And hating it.

'Five days. Starting now. You're owed about two months' holiday because you never take it. They're *telling* you to take it. Call in on the top brass on your way out. You're to do nothing but eat, walk and sleep.'

'You're joking?'

'Nope. Pack your bags and take a break. See you after the R & R, mate. Enjoy the time out because you deserve it.'

Abbott didn't even argue.

9
Day 2

JOLTED FROM HIS MEMORIES, Abbott looked up at the clock. At long last, after the fingers had slowed almost to a standstill, it was time. He took the small bunch of keys from the empty desk drawer and placed them in an inner pocket of his rucksack and checked and re-checked that they were zipped in. Barely a thought had he spared for the lock they fitted, nor for the door of the hut they opened. Barely a thought since his only aunt had died, without a husband or children, the previous year.

Then, when she lay in her hospice bed, her skin like rice paper, she had placed these same keys, linked by a chain to a silver dolphin, in the palm of his hand.

'I always loved it,' she said. 'You have it now. The sea's in your blood too.'

'The beach hut,' he'd replied, inadequately. 'Thank

you. I remember it from my visits when I was a kid. You went there often, didn't you?'

'Yes. My refuge. My real home. I felt truly myself there.' Her words were frayed, her breath coming in gasps. 'I didn't *visit*. I lived there whenever I could. There's the dinghy too of course....' She could manage no more. She enclosed his hand and the keys, squeezing with a faint pressure, and closed her eyes. Then in a whisper, 'I'm sorry I forgot all about it in the will…you'll need to change the deeds…'

'Don't worry. I'll sort it out. Thank you,' he said, kissing her on the forehead, knowing she had only days left and would never see the hut or the sea again.

And afterwards, in the car park, through tears, *What the fuck do I want with a beach hut in a sad little seaside resort?*

Because it was a legacy from a woman he'd respected and loved very much, he had hesitated about starting up the wheels of the legal juggernaut which would alter her will and make right the omission. The keys stayed in his desk. He neither visited the place nor picked up the phone to a solicitor to set in motion the business of selling it. Perhaps he didn't want it to belong to someone else. If only she knew now how true and valuable a gift she had given him. He longed to tell her that it would be *his* refuge. A safe house. A hiding place. Sure, they'd catch up with him eventually but it gave him precious time to think, to work out a plan, to come to terms with the inevitable changes ahead. He knew his guilt was magnified and multiplied by the act of running away, but he would not stick around in a heated climate of revenge in which the brutally culpable and cruel were rightly hunted down and shamed, and a few – yes, a few who perhaps did not deserve the humiliation and punishment – were nailed on the same homophobic crucifix.

And there was the sea. If he decided that a police cell and a court case packed with sensation-seeking journos was not an option he could cope with, there was the sea. He could walk. He could take out the dinghy and let it drift back by itself.

Aw, come off it. Get a grip, Abbott. There's no need to write a soap with a suicide at the end of an episode. This story is about a bloke who left his computer logged on and had the sheer bad luck of some homo-hater hacking it. Crass stupidity. Not serious crime and melodrama.

At ten forty-five, he jammed a dark cap low over his forehead and shrugged his bulk into a long army coat even though the night was warm. He knew where the apartment building's CCTV cameras were and he also knew that half the time they were broken or switched off. This might be his lucky night. Leaving his car locked in the drive, its keys stowed in his pocket, he quietly closed his front door and set off, taking the short cut through night-dark woods to the train station. Emerging on the high street, he took a brief detour to the bank, keyed in his PIN and withdrew five hundred pounds. That should do for a while. There would be other banks in towns a bus ride or two from the resort. At the train station he used the automatic vending machine to buy an open ticket to a resort on the coast eighty miles beyond his actual destination.

That'll keep them guessing for a day or two. Then he sighed. *Nothing I'm doing will keep them guessing. Who are you kidding? This is child's play.*

Anyone watching – and who was at this hour – would have seen a strong, well built man struggling nevertheless with an awkwardly stuffed, heavy holdall that banged against his legs with every step, and a back-pack that pressed into his shoulder muscles. They would have assumed he was off on his holidays and might wonder why he'd chosen such an unsociable hour and why he hadn't bought himself some decent luggage.

10
Day 2

T HE MINUTES WERE HOURS and the hours were days as the train slogged its way across the flat black landscape of the east coast and clunked through small towns lit by neon signs that flashed and were gone. Finally it took a sharp, rolling turn to the left and started its coastline rattle, stopping at unseen stations where notice boards marked a place, and another place, where life had ceased until dawn. Abbott sat in an empty carriage, his bags at his feet, his head bowed, too wrung out to think any more about the consequences of his actions. Much later, he would acknowledge the absurdity of his flight but for the time being the adrenalin fuel tank had run empty, leaving his mind a void where the residue of emotions slid in and slid out, like the tide briefly washing up against a rock worn to a glassy smoothness and rolling away again.

The sign that marked his destination came as a shock. The place still existed. The train *did* stop here. He would not ride in limbo forever. When the train creaked and dragged itself to a halt, he lurched upright, heaved up his bags and stumbled out into another dead, deserted place marked only by a name. Standing on the platform, he looked at the sign and was taken by surprise at the flood of long-ago memories and images triggered by the unmistakable smell of the sea; a seaweed saltiness that hung heavy in the air. As a boy, he'd come in school holidays to stay with his aunt in her cottage a few miles away and had found her quiet, undemanding, uncritical company easy and relaxing. The two of them had spent most days on the beach in companionable silence, both treading the sand, heads down, out in all weathers searching for treasures; taking back a bleached, time-warped chunk of drift wood or a piece of green sea glass, both always glancing up at the ever-changing pastel palette of sky and sea. When the light faded, they turned back to the hut where they would spend the night. After a casserole or fish and chips, they sat wrapped in tartan rugs on the tiny verandah, sipping hot chocolate and watching the night complete its darkening. Then the boat lights popped on one by one until, on a clear night, they became swaying land-stars that cast runny reflections in the waves as the boats tilted in the wind.

The visits had petered out when the boy became an

adolescent and there were more compelling things to do than visit an ageing aunt in a dated seaside town. Ibiza and Greece and Morocco called. With his mates and girlfriends, he jostled the crowds on churning ferries and boarded over-heated buses and hitched across Europe. Gaudy market stalls and late night discos and bars that sold substances stronger than beer made them giddy with carefree, eternal youth. The beach hut faded into an almost forgotten relic of a boyhood past. Yet here he was, twenty-five years later, back on the same territory.

At this hour there were of course no taxis, which was fine because to show his face would have been risky. It was less than three miles to the beach and after sitting rigid and tense with the rattle of clickety-click wheels in his ears, he needed the walk and the fresh air even with his ludicrously unwieldy luggage. The main road, at first a long lonely stretch of nothingness, reached B&B land, then sprouted arteries to the left which wound downhill towards and through the town centre: past the tourist shops, their stands of t-shirts and flip-flops pulled inside behind shutters for the night, past Tesco Lifestyle, past pizza places where faded photos of meals cello-taped in the windows told the punters what they could eat, past hairdressers and nail bars and betting shops and slot machine arcades. Neon lights gave the place a garish pallor and made it sadly old-fashioned, though perhaps by daylight it would look just the same. It didn't matter. He would live facing away from all of this, venturing up the hill from the promenade only for provisions. The summer would soon be gone and the shops and cafes would close until the following year. The resort would die, leaving the old folk who always lived here and the dwindling numbers of families and single men who could find winter work. The young left for the big cities the minute the doors closed on their school careers. Better to stack shelves than to stay here.

At the bottom of the hill, a line of bollards marked the end of access to vehicles and the start of the concrete pedestrian promenade that ran above the beach, giving access to the sands every fifty or so metres down a flight of steps. The stalls dotted along the way, like the shops, were shut up for the night, but he noted that this was where he could come for easy food when he didn't feel like preparing meals himself. Half-way along the promenade, a brightly coloured wall rose up, surprising visitors who had expected to see discreet shades of cream and white. A relic from another era, these beach huts had acquired an unexpected nostalgia and popularity, had been gentrified, and were valued by town folk and holiday makers alike. His aunt's was the last but one. She had always wanted to paint it a deep turquoise to match the sea on the sunniest day but the rules for cosmetic changes to the exterior were strict and many. Seven colours were permitted and turquoise wasn't one of them, so red it stayed. Yes, there it was.

There's no-one watching, you idiot. Not a soul on the beach but you, he told himself without conviction as he walked along the concrete, placing one careful foot in front of the other and holding his holdall in both arms so that it did not make a noise banging against his legs. His arm muscles screamed. No light shone from any of the huts below and he knew that apart from his aunt, people did not sleep in them. At least they hadn't when he was a kid. But fear and lack of sleep dumbed down reason and he told himself someone might be staying the night.

Students. Squatters. Someone eccentric like my aunt. Someone on the run like me.

Reaching the farthest end where there were no more steps, he hung his bag and rucksack from the ends of his aching arms, as far as he could reach, before letting go. He winced as they landed with barely a thump. Then he bent his knees and jumped, aiming for the quietest possible landing on the sand. The very soft thud made his heart race and he waited at the end of the line of huts for several minutes before moving or poking his head round the corner. A fleeting glimpse.

Nothing. Nobody.

The end hut where he was now standing had the luxury of a side window and with a brief look inside, he reassured himself that this one was definitely empty. He looked in again for longer. Deck chairs and small tables were folded and stacked against the far wall, and other stuff was packed away in boxes, suggesting the owners had left and might not be back this season. It looked too neat and tidy and swept to be a quick end-of-day clearance before another day on the beach. He picked up his bags and began a breath-held walk from the end hut to his own. Yes, his own. In his pocket, he felt for the keys on their dolphin chain.

It was with guilty, worried speed that he fumbled the key into the lock, pushed open the red door and got himself and his bags inside. Five seconds. He closed the door very softly behind him and for the first time since he'd come back from lunch to find his computer hacked, he let his shoulders droop. Leaning against the door, he closed his eyes and permitted himself a slow outward breath of relief. Whatever happened, he had a few days of precious time here to think it through, to reflect on the magnitude of what he'd done and to come to terms with whatever consequences might follow. But right now, in this red cell, they didn't matter. *Now* mattered. The very early hours of today mattered. And tomorrow – when it came. And the next day.

With weary, travel-sore eyes, he looked around. Apart from the musty unused smell of a hut that had been shut up for more than a year and the layer of fine sand that had blown under the crack below the door and covered every surface, this interior was a work of domestic perfection, its confined space converted into a workable, delightful home. Like a small caravan, or a camper van, only more lived-in and private. Every detail had been considered.

Against the farthest wall was a platform holding a mattress with folded bedding on top and book shelves below. His aunt's books still packed one half of the rough wooden planks while the rest of the space was filled with wicker baskets, probably for clothes, which exactly slotted into the spaces. A full-length red curtain was pushed to one side, but could be drawn across the bed, maybe to separate night from day. At the front, a window above a table was hung with the same filmy red fabric and a blind could also be pulled down to stop the light leaking out, light from a genuine old oil lamp because there was no electricity.

Peeling his body from the security of the door, Abbott went to the window, pulled down the blind and closed the curtains. His aunt had been clear-thinking enough to have left matches next to the lamp. Abbott lifted the glass cover, turned up the wick, struck a match and held it close. Little beads of fire sizzled around the wick before flaring confidently into creamy flames which he turned down and tuned to a rich, pulsing glow that filled the space with welcoming light.

For a while he explored – opening doors and pulling out drawers and marvelling at the satisfying completion of it all. On one side was a compact kitchen with a gas-fired two ring hob and a roomy cool box. He made a mental note to buy ice. A cupboard below held basic cooking utensils and crockery, and cutlery stood ready in an earthenware jar. On the beach side, below the window, the small table and chair stood ready for eating, for reading, for staring at the view. It was blocked at the moment by the two deck chairs leaning against it, but they could be stacked somewhere else. On the walls were maps of the area with walks marked in green felt tip and notes in the margins which commented on particular places and sights. *Dolphins here,* one said. *Wild orchids in this meadow,* said another. And *Walked this cliff top in a Force 8.* Above the desk were photographs of his aunt, his parents and himself. A very young self.

Enough. Plenty. He'd seen all that he needed to and knew it would be perfect. It took another five minutes for him to place a pillow at the curtained end of the bed, spread a sheet and a duvet – never mind a cover for what was left of tonight – climb up, register the firm comfortable mattress and fall into a deep dreamless sleep.

A long time later, or so it seemed, lines of bright light playing in the cracks of the blind and on either side of the red gauze curtain woke him and told him that the sun was already high in the sky.

11
Day 3

CAFFEINE WAS MORE urgent than unpacking so he rummaged in his bag for the plain, navy peaked cap and pulled it down over his forehead. He would never exit without it. Nor the long dark coat which was both unfashionable and impractical for an English beach, but it served as camouflage. There were strong plastic bags on a hook by the door which he folded and stuffed into his pocket. Playing the role of a man who lived a normal, ordinary life here, staying for a few days to take a break and unwind, he unlocked the door, locked it behind him and walked as casually as he could manage across the tiny verandah and down the three steps to the sand. The hut at the end of the row still looked packed up and closed. As he walked past the others, glancing as casually as he could towards the sea then briefly back to their brightly coloured fronts, he made a quick judgement that all except one was deserted. The third one from the promenade steps had chairs and a small table on the verandah. An empty mug stood by the door as if forgotten the evening before, and the curtains were open. People were expected.

He ducked his head as he entered Tesco, pretending to search in his pocket for change. The CCTV camera over the entrance would get a shot of the top of a cap.

Damn the constant vigil over every ordinary citizen. Damn our complete loss of privacy.

He heard Jim's instant reply.

You didn't say that when CCTV helped us out, mate. When it sent us images of boys who'd gone off radar.

Abbott allowed himself the smallest smile. *Bugger off, Jim. I'm on the other side of the fence now.*

Into his basket he tossed a couple of packets of ground coffee, muesli, UHT milk, bread, butter, jam, fruit, packets of ham and cheese. Keep it simple. And several bottles of ordinary red wine and bars of good black chocolate. To his surprise and satisfaction, Tesco even sold big bags of ice cubes, maybe to keep the campers happy by keeping their beer cold on warm English nights. He used the automatic check-out, paid in cash and was gone in less than fifteen minutes, walking back towards the beach, a slight spring in his step after completing his first simple practical task. *Without being caught.* OK, it was a joke, but only just. He had the basics to live for a few days. *And God knows how many days I have.*

From the steps that led from the promenade to the beach, he could see a stir of activity on the verandah of the hut which looked like it was still being used. A man was sitting in one of two white plastic chairs, facing the sea, unfolding a tabloid newspaper and a woman was walking in and out, finally emerging with two steaming mugs. She sat beside him.

Look like they're in their early 60s. Retired maybe. Please let them be private people.

Walking purposefully yet casually, he did his best to pass them without drawing attention to himself, turning his head sharply away when he drew even as if something caught his eye way out to sea.

'Lovely morning!' shouted the bloke on cue. He had on khaki shorts with a pleat that would cut your finger. His stocky body was a mahogany criss-cross of weather lines fuzzed with grey hair. Out of a ruddy face, small currant eyes openly stared at Abbott as if a foreigner was crossing home soil.

Damn!

'Lovely!' Abbott replied, still walking, not intending to stop.

'Down for the day, are you? Going to spend it in one of the huts?' called the woman.

Abbott ignored the question.

'Nice day for it. Not seen you around before.'

Fuck!

She was in jogger pants and a large t-shirt with a glittery heart. *Obviously not here for the swimming,* Abbott thought, then felt ashamed of himself for the cruel judgment. The orange shade of her face might have been make-up or too many hours sitting here in the wind and sun.

'Staying long are you?'

None of your damn business. Bloody neighbourhood watch.

'Just a few days.' No option but to reply. His carrier bags were hanging from his fingers, biting into the flesh.

'The red one?'

He hesitated but of course they knew. 'Yes.'

'We thought so. An elderly woman used to come and stay there but we've not seen her for ages. I hope she's OK,' the woman continued. And when Abbott didn't reply, she added, 'She was friendly but kept herself to herself. You know what I mean?' He refused to give her what she wanted so on she went. 'We live up in the town. On the estate. Not many days left now for the hut,' she said, scanning the sky as if expecting rain from the settled pale sky.

Yup! Bring it on! A Shakespearean storm that will send you running.

'No. I suppose not.'

'We might pack up end of this week. We'll see.'

Let there be gales and hurricanes.

'Are you on holiday? Lovely beach, isn't it?'

No, I'm hiding from the police, Madam. I'm on some list of hard porn punters or worse, gay pedophiles who work with boys. I'm a criminal.

'Sort of. I'm writing a book and need some peace and quiet.'

'Oh that's interesting. What are you writing?' she asked, while the man stared and sipped his coffee. Abbott, hungry and longing for a triple espresso, could smell cheap milky instant and almost gagged.

'A novel.'

'I like poetry,' she replied. 'Wordsworth. You know that one about the daffodils…'

'Name's Sinclair,' the man interrupted, perhaps not wanting a recital. 'Bill and Ida. Lived in the town for fifteen years. Been coming down here to the hut for ten. If you need to know anything, just ask. We know most folk and what's going on.'

I bet.

'What do we call you then?' Bill asked when nothing was offered in return.

'Mace,' Abbott said, perhaps prompted by the colour of the sand because he had completely forgotten to think up a name. 'Phil Mace.' Then quickly, hoping the name hadn't registered, 'Anything in the paper today?' Abbott tried to read the big print of the Daily Mail without appearing to, expecting a headline shouting: SUSPECT YOUTH WORKER VANISHES.

Too soon! They'll expect me to turn up and face the music, especially if Jim has assured them I will. No headlines yet.

'Nice to meet you, Phil. No, nothing much in the paper. I get it mostly for the sport.'

'Well, I'll leave you to your coffee and get this lot back and unpacked before the ice melts,' he said, trying hard to soften the matching ice in his voice. Not wanting to arouse the slightest hostility or suspicion.

'See you around,' Bill said. 'If the weather's good, we'll be here for a few more days, as the wife said. If the hut's locked up, we've gone.'

The sooner the better.

Abbott lifted his carrier bags from the sand where he'd finally parked them while he was kept talking and continued on his way, freeing a hand to wave from a few yards further on. When he climbed the steps to the red hut, a glimpse back told him two pairs of eyes were watching him.

Damn!

Depleted and drained from the strain of monitoring every word he spoke, and from the prying and nosiness disguised as small talk, he managed only to stack the deck chairs outside before shutting the door on the world. Then he did nothing until the pan of water had boiled and he'd made a cafetiere of very strong coffee. While its rich aroma floated round the hut, he cut and buttered three thick slabs of wholemeal bread and spread them with blueberry jam. He carried it all to the table and, after pulling open the curtains a few inches, sank into the leather-seated upright chair. The first hot gulp of coffee was sheer sensual bliss. The first bite of sweet bread a feast. His breathing slowed.

When finally he swivelled in his chair, he let his eyes wander inch by inch, detail by detail over what would be his home for a few days, maybe with luck longer, and thanked his aunt for creating this space. As a boy he'd been oblivious of its unique charm, coming only for a day and racing out barefoot within minutes of arriving to the sand, the rocks and the sea. The privacy of the interior, its comfort and harmony, had passed him by.

He unpacked what he'd brought, stowing his clothes in the wicker baskets on the shelves and the contents of his briefcase in the drawers under the table. It was only when he had extracted his laptop and inserted the adaptor that, holding the flex and plug and bending down below the table, he remembered there was no electricity. *How we take things for granted,* he thought with a smile. Initial disappointment faded to a sense of relief and freedom. Like being willingly cut adrift. He didn't even open the lid. Didn't check the battery. Not for a moment did he consider going in search of an internet cafe, not that there'd be one. Not here. It was far better not to know than to be anxiously checking Jim's emails. The laptop went back in the briefcase. The briefcase was put away, out of sight. Out of mind. What would be…

With a perceptible upturn of mood, he moved across and knelt beside the books. Local history, archeology, biographies, novels, poetry – so much carefully chosen reading which would occupy his mind at night. Maybe even calm it. How long was it since he'd read a book? He didn't notice that an hour had passed.

Instead of site jumping and skim-reading the Guardian Online, he pottered about the hut, unpacking his last belongings and squashing his bags into a small empty cupboard where they would not remind him of journeys. He collected and put outside the big shells, collected perhaps by a younger self long ago but which now spoke of dusty souvenirs on suburban shelves. Feeling bold, he dumped his notepad and a pencil on the table just in case. Just in case the words that span around his head came together in coherent lines. Prose or poetry. Doggerel. Notes. It didn't matter. He made another cafetiere of coffee and carried it to the table. The sharp edges of his panic faded into something more like background noise which he could ignore for long moments. Even his answers to the endlessly repeated question – *why did you bolt like a criminal* – sounded off-key and distant. The orchestra that played them had grown tired or had forgotten the notes. The counterpoint arguments, spoken in Jim's persuasive voice, still broke in but with less insistence, telling him to come back, to get on the next train, that it was all a big mistake and a huge over-reaction. Sipping from a hand-thrown white mug and comfortable in the leather cushioned chair, he located his mind's OFF button and stared at the horizon and the soothingly, repetitively choreographed movement of the waves. He'd deal with all the other stuff in his own time.

Finally, sleep overcoming him, he moved to the bed. Folded at the foot of the mattress where he'd thrown himself down in the middle of the night, he found a white sheet, red duvet cover and pillow cases. It was tricky crawling around on all fours in the confined space, banging his head on the ceiling, but he managed to make up the bed. Not perfect with hospital folded corners, but good enough. His. When he lay down on it, arms folded behind his head, he felt something close to peace. Resignation perhaps. A sense of an ending.

When he woke from an hour's coma-like sleep, it took a few minutes for the confusion to roll away and for his memory to catch up. From the brightness of the light in the rectangle of window not veiled by red curtains, he knew the sun was high in a blue sky. The slooshing wash of the tide and the fainter scuttle of pebbles at the sea's edge was rhythmic and inevitable. He lay for a while longer, telling himself to stop playing the tape loop now and to listen to the other sounds, to stop the self-recrimination, to let go of the guilt and let things be.

You can't do anything else. Face the music when the band arrives. Until then, live quietly with the sea.

It was about five-twenty, after a gentle afternoon of wiping the accumulation of sand from surfaces and sweeping it from the floor, when he emerged. He'd made the hut's close acquaintance by touching and holding and valuing what it held. A Russian-doll cradle of wooden spoons, each one snug inside the next. Bowl-shaped, deep purple wine glasses. Paperback books with scuffed corners that had obviously been read. By the end of the afternoon, he felt like he and the hut accepted one another. They had reached an agreement. When he opened the door, a glance along the row of huts reassured him that the Neighbourhood Watch had gone home and that he had the beach pretty much to himself. Feet in scuffed old trainers, his cap pulled low, he set off across hard-packed sand towards the sea, breathing in the seaweed-dank, salt-tang air and feeling a strong tug towards the hypnotic, monotonous movement of the tide on the turn, making its way out to sea and dragging with it sand and stones and human detritus. And his past.

On his way back from the cove at the end, he noticed a single small figure near the shore line. A boy, aged maybe seven or eight with a shock of hair that he kept pushing back off his face, stood with otherwise unusual stillness, poised, looking at the boats. Perhaps he was waiting for one to chug to the shore and pick him up. A fisherman's son? No, he'd be waiting on the pier. *A bit young to be out alone,* Abbott wondered. Then, *Don't even think about it.*

In the heavier, heel-clinging sand nearer the shore, he was content to linger, taking his time to register the curve of the bay, the ugly background scramble of buildings on the promenade, and the drifting line of the horizon which would very soon be obscured. On he went, turning once, perhaps twenty yards on. The boy was looking straight at him and for a second their eyes locked. A small hand was pulled from a pocket and tentatively raised, ready to offer a short wave. It came. Abbott lifted his arm and waved back. Then walked on. It was nothing. Nothing at all.

12
Day 4

WHEN HE WOKE on the second day, Abbott sensed his revved up energy had shifted down through the gears, calmed and quietened by the womb-like space. The sand in the hourglass poured more slowly and the sun took longer to cross the sky. It surprised him that he could adapt this easily from the tension and pressure of interviews and counselling and court cases and rushed sandwiches and late nights at his desk, a way of life that had lasted fifteen years, to a solitude that was accompanied only by the in and out wash of the waves and the call of gulls. The sea breathed its way up the beach, wave by fluttering wave, to the ragged seaweed mark in the sand where it frothed quietly for a while, then just as inevitably began its retreat.

But the lull didn't last. By mid morning he was staring at reality, replaying the tape loops until his emotions were raw and troubling. He couldn't sit still. With too much caffeine in his veins, and its after effects in his bladder, he left the hut to take a leak. And to make short sorties along the beach, always turning to the left, towards the rocks. The muscle power needed to tread through the thick sand dispersed some of the nervous energy. The sound of the sea blocked some of the insistent monologues.

There were fewer people on the beach, fewer still on spread towels. The sun was weaker and a hint of autumnal chill blew in from the sea. It would not be long before, apart from dog-walkers and fresh air fanatics and joggers, the place would be empty. The boy hadn't come back. Engaging with him had been stupid but it didn't matter. *Probably some kid on holiday who's gone home now.* By lunch time, he'd let it go. And by lunch time he was hungry and had no bread.

The Sinclairs were installed on their deck wearing bright fleeces. Like lifeguards on look out duty. The choice was to avoid them by heading straight to the sea and then walking close to the shoreline before heading up again to the promenade or to walk straight past them. The first would arouse more suspicion and raise hackles. The second would lead to unwanted conversation. A rock and a hard place.

'Not so nice today,' Ida called, turning to face Abbott as he drew level. 'Bit on the chilly side but it should warm up later.'

He nodded an acknowledgement and kept walking.

'Settling in OK?' She was standing now and moving towards the railings. Bill looked up from The Mail.

'Yes, thank you.'

'Going to the shops are you?'

No. The race course. The Hilton. A brothel. A bloody police station to hand myself in.

'Tesco is good. Nice snacks and sandwiches if you're staying another night or two in the hut.'

Another nod. The woman was not subtle.

'We were talking about you last night, Bill and me, and I wanted to make sure I asked you if you needed anything. Can't be easy living by yourself in that hut.'

'I'm fine, thanks.' There was no avoiding looking in their direction. He stopped mid-stride and flicked his eyes over the huge headlines.

'The same bloody awful news,' Bill said, not missing a trick. 'Country's going to the dogs. Immigrants coming to Europe by the ferry load. Serves them right if they drown on the way.'

Jesus. The tabloids hit the spot all right.

Abbott gave the merest nod.

'This country's over-run. We don't have room for all these foreigners. Take this place… it's filling up with Poles. Farage is getting my vote next week even though I've been a Tory voter all my life. They come here in droves, take our jobs, move into our houses, use our NHS, sign up for benefits. This country isn't English any more.'

Abbott swallowed a gutter full of words. So Bill didn't just read the sports pages.

'Bill's in a bad mood today,' Ida added. 'We just heard coloureds are moving into the empty flat next to ours. Not that I've got anything against coloureds, only there's too many of them here already. Indians. Pakistanis. And Muslims pretending to pray in mosques when they're plotting to blow up our airports and trains and tubes. We don't need that. We don't need to be frightened every time we travel anywhere.'

'There can't be many immigrants here. They go to the big cities to find work.' *Not to this jobless half-dead seaside dot on the map.* He had to speak.

'Oh you'd be surprised how many foreigners live here.' Her tone was self-righteousness.

'The news is shocking. Immigrants and perverts.' Bill's turn. 'All this stuff about Jimmy Savile messing with kids, poor sods.' Bill took his eyes off The Mail and pinned Abbott to the spot with his stare. 'And there we were thinking what a good man he was. Remember *Jim'll Fix It*? And him running marathons to raise money. Stoke Mandeville. And all the time he was doing horrible things. Kids in wheelchairs. Kids with a few screws loose. And not just him. Others. Household names. People we admired and watched on the telly.'

Abbott spoke into the brief pause. A mere, 'Yes.'

'We're too tolerant. Gay Pride and all that.' He shook his head. 'Men holding hands. Kissing. And now bloody weddings.' He slammed the paper down on the table.

Ida gave Abbott a quick sheepish look, as if her husband had stepped over an invisible line. Abbott said nothing.

He had heard it all so many times before, working with the kids. Homosexuality was such a familiar scapegoat and a much cited blind alley. Blame the queers. Blame same-sex relationships even if they've lasted twenty years and are more loving than many straight ones. Normally he could blank it off, but here, in this claustrophobic little town, expressed out loud a few doors away from his own, these views were dangerous. Politically dangerous and personally dangerous. He bit his lip. Did his cap hide his frown?

'Don't mind Bill. He's just letting off steam because of us getting neighbours we don't want. He did complain but the council took no notice so he's miffed.' Ida sighed. 'I understand how he feels. He doesn't want the smell of curry wafting in every day and women with their faces covered up so you can't see what they're thinking.' She waited for acknowledgement and acceptance but none came.

'Are your new neighbours Muslim?' he asked.

'Haven't a clue. We just know they're not white. Anyway… not English.'

Perhaps they're as British as you are. And

compassionate. And open-minded.

'Oh well…never mind…' She paused, thrown by his silence. 'We was also talking about the lady that used to live in the red hut. I asked you yesterday, remember, but I don't think you said…quite elderly but kept herself to herself. We used to worry about her. Wondered how much longer she'd be able to manage. I said to Bill last night, maybe she's your mother.' It was a question.

So they'd been discussing him. Well, what else did they have to do?

'No,' he replied, refusing to give her more.

'Oh. A relative?' she prodded.

'Just someone I know. I'd better get going. I need bread for lunch.'

There was a definite exchange of looks that told him, as clearly as if they'd said it, that he'd been given a black mark. He was not one of them. Tightened lips and narrowed eyes spoke their disapproval. Perhaps he imagined it, but he sniffed suspicion.

'Well, we'll still be here when you come back,' Bill said.

Too damn right you will. Just what I need, two people with empty lives sitting here watching me and swilling hatred for gay men, blacks and Muslims.

'Not very friendly, is he?' Ida said, when he was a few yards away, loud enough for him to hear.'

'Doesn't want to give us the time of day,' Bill replied.

'Oh well… maybe he's too busy thinking about that book he's writing.'

13
Day 3

B ACK FROM THE SHOPS and unsettled after his latest encounter with the Sinclairs, Abbott left the hut again several times to pace back and forth along the dry sand high up the beach, repeatedly reminding himself that he was over-reacting. They were a bloody nuisance, but they couldn't hurt him. The effort of lifting his legs higher than on any urban walk produced aches in undiscovered muscles but a quietening of his churning thoughts. Later, after too many chunks of crusty bread and brie, he had climbed up on the bed to read Ted Hughes, but the words and sentences gradually ran into one another to be absorbed by the soothing rhythmic slap and slurp of the tide and he'd slept deeply. Afternoon naps were becoming a relaxing habit.

When he left the hut at five-fifteen, still sleep-drugged and lost in half-remembered dreams in which fingers played on pianos that turned into giant keyboards, he didn't register the boy sitting under his window with his back against the hut wall.

Oh for heaven's sake.

'*Please* can I go for a walk with you?'

'No. I want to walk by myself. Go away. You're not to come here.' Caught unaware, he didn't temper his exasperation or disguise his anger. The boy looked up. Tears welled in his grey eyes. 'That's two people in twelve minutes who've told me to go away,' he said wretchedly.

'Well, people don't want you hanging around all the time.'

'It isn't all the time. It's the second time.'

'Whatever. People want to be left in peace. They don't always want to talk to a child. Sorry, but that's how it is and maybe you'd better learn. Leave people alone. OK?'

'And the other man shouted at me. He said he'd call Social Services,' the boy continued, as if Abbott hadn't spoken. He'd kept the man's angry words bottled up and needed to say them out loud.

'Which man?'

'The one in the white hut. And I don't talk to people 'cause mum says I mustn't talk to strangers.'

'Quite right.' The irony made him smile.

'They were staring at me and looking cross so I said Hello and the man said Go away. Same as you.' The boy hung his head.

'Oh dear.'

'And then the man said, I'm going to report you, son. Night after night you're out here by yourself for hours on end. It's not right. Social Services will be interested to hear about it. How old are you anyway? but I didn't tell him. And it's not hours on end, it's an hour and a half. And not every evening, just when Mum's working.' He got to his feet and shrugged his shoulders several times. Up and down, up and down. Wiped his face with the back of his sandy hand. Returned both hands to his pockets. Looked utterly dejected.

Abbott paused.

Them again. Bloody Vigilante. Blacks, Muslims, Gays. Now boys on beaches.

As Abbott marched down the steps he couldn't help but throw out the obvious question, maybe because the boy had lumped him in with the dreadful Sinclairs. 'Well…why *are* you out alone?' A twinge of sympathy as well as curiosity scuppered his impulse to get rid of the lad. Plus his growing dislike for the man who looked the type to make trouble. Now, apparently, for a scrap of a kid. 'Haven't you got a home?'

Running alongside to keep up, his breath coming in quick gasps, the boy was only too eager to offer an explanation. '*Of course* I've got a home but my mum works at five o'clock…and I go for a walk by myself…and then I buy a cone of chips and eat them and then I go home.'

Abbott kept up the punishing pace as if to shake off the child at his side. 'What does she do? Your mother?'

'Men come to the house and she talks to them. She cheers them up and then they pay her. She dresses up in her sparkly clothes first.'

So that's why the child walks on the beach.

'Every day? Do you go for a walk by yourself every day?'

'Not every day. Most days.'

'And you don't mind?'

'No. I like walking by myself. Except when someone's nasty to me.' He pulled a face and bit his lip.

'Nasty? Like who?'

'Well, that man and woman in the white hut are nasty. He told me he was going to report me. For being alone. Without my mum.' He put out a hand and touched the sleeve of Abbott's coat. 'I don't want my mum in trouble 'cause she's not done anything wrong. Those people already got her into trouble.'

Abbott glanced down. Slowed his steps. The child seemed desperate to talk.

'What did they do to your mum?'

'She used to work with her friend, Janie. They both worked at our house at five o'clock. But the police came round. That man in the white hut had told on them...'

'How do you know it was him?'

'My mum said it was him. The police said my mum

had to work by herself or it was a… a… can't think of the name.' The boy sighed loudly.

Brothel. More than one sex worker and the place of work is classified as a brothel. Even if it's two sisters. Or two friends working together. For their own safety. Damn Sinclair.

'OK. I understand. Was your mum upset?'

'Yup. She cried. For a while no men came and I didn't go for walks.' His face crumpled into anxiety. 'But you see we don't have enough money so she had to start again.'

Ah. So that was it.

Now he understood the solitary walks and the world weariness. It was another familiar story, though the boys he'd dealt with had been older and their mums turned them out on to brutal city streets where they'd found gangs and drugs and crime. Where they'd stood on corners dealing. And become addicts themselves.

The poor little blighter. Not much trouble for him to get into here though, not walking up and down a flat English beach. Tedious maybe, but not dangerous. Especially with two bored, unpleasant people watching his every move.

He looked down at the troubled face and slowed his pace to a gentle walk.

'What happened after that?'

'She waited a bit and didn't do her work. Then she started again on her own. But I think she's a bit scared.' He sounded matter of fact, as if he shared and shouldered his mother's concern.

'I see.'

'Only this time if the police come it'll be my fault 'cause I annoyed that man in the white hut.'

They walked on, Abbott no longer trying to shed the child.

'The police won't come again.'

'You sure?' His head was tilted as he walked close to Abbott's side and stared up at him.

'Positive.' It was a lie but the boy needed to be let off the hook.

It was like a weight had been lifted. The boy's steps became lighter. More bouncy. On they went, side by side, not talking, until Abbott was back where he'd been for the last fifteen years, once again doing his work, questioning a troubled boy.

'Do you have any brothers or sisters?'

'No.'

'Your dad?'

'Just me and mum.'

'Dad left?'

'I never had a dad.'

Of course. A single parent working the only way available to her.

'I'll talk to the man.' A reflex. The words slipped out despite his ticking time bomb of a situation, despite his need for complete privacy. It would have been against his nature to do otherwise.

Sensing a softening, the boy hooked his arm through

the man's and on they went, a companionable silence replacing the boy's palpable anxiety until Abbott heard him counting his steps in a small whisper. *Two hundred and one, two hundred and two…* until they came to a halt at the entrance to the next cove.

'Less than usual,' the boy said.

'What's less than usual?'

'The number of steps.'

'Well…we were walking fast. Especially at the beginning.'

'I know.' Quiet satisfaction replaced the slight concern.

For a while they watched the heave of water up against the rocks and the fountain of spray falling from the tops back into the chaos of the confused pools below. The sea slapped itself round in circles, dark and dangerous.

'I wouldn't want to be in the water here,' Abbott said, as much to himself as to the boy. He was a strong swimmer but had a healthy respect for the sea.

'I can't swim.'

'No-one's taught you?'

'No. Mum can't swim either.'

'Yet you live here with it next door.'

'Not next door!'

The man smiled. Always so literal.

'Well…I suppose you can't swim by yourself in the evenings anyway so what do you do?'

'The same things. I like things to be the same. I always

walk to here, look at the rocks and… sometimes…' he looked up, hesitating before trusting the man with his next words. 'I search hard for a mermaid… just in case… and then I walk back.'

'A mermaid,' Abbott repeated, not colouring the word with any judgement. The boy must be seven or eight. *Did he really believe in mermaids?*

The boy heard the unvoiced question. 'Oh, I know they're not real but I've read in books that they call men in boats to their death on rocks like these… dangerous jagged rocks where the current is very strong and… um… stir crazy.' He looked at the man to see if he was laughing, but his face was serious and he had even bent his head to listen. 'I like to check. Just suppose there was a mermaid and she sang to a small fishing boat and it got into trouble here, I could run for help. I'd love to help the fishermen 'cause when we buy their fish on the quay they knock down the price. Two pounds instead of two pounds fifty. And I wouldn't tell anyone about the mermaid.'

Thank God this boy had an imagination to help while away the hours when he made the same journey along the beach with no-one to talk to and no-one to hear the stories he told himself to spill a little magic into a strained, solitary existence.

'That was a silly thing to say, wasn't it?' he asked, his voice quieter. 'Stupid, really.'

'No.' Abbott replied. 'Who says there are no mermaids?' And the boy looked at him with ingenuous trust and gratitude.

When they turned around to head back, two pairs of eyes were drawn to the exact same spot.

'Gone,' the boy said. 'They've usually gone by now.'

'Yes.'

'But…if they're there tomorrow…and if we go for a walk together, then I'm not alone, am I? And they won't report me?'

The boy searched the man's face for approval of his plan and Abbott, against his better judgement, found himself warming to the childish suggestion of a comradely union against a common foe. Linking up with this untainted soul appealed to his wish to take a stand against sour and spiteful convention. Not what he needed, though. Not what he wanted. Bloody stupid, really.

And how do I explain knowing the boy? And how come we're buddies? Because sure as hell, they'll poke and pry and ask.

The answer came unprompted.

None of their bloody business.

Back at the red hut, the boy made no attempt to continue the togetherness. He let go of the man's hand and walked on with sure, sprightly steps, turning just once to raise his hand and wave. When Abbott poked his head out ten minutes later to look at the stars which flared in the clear, almost-black sky and to find Orion, he could see a small shape sitting on the wall, swinging skinny legs. It was too dark to see but Abbott guessed he was eating his chips. Eating and counting. Counting each chip before he chewed and swallowed it.

14
Day 6

'ARE *YOU* A STRANGER?' he asked, matter-of-fact, twisting round from his seat on the bottom step. A concentric circle of pebbles curled round and round from large to small like a snails's shell. 'Twenty-four,' he said, 'but I can't find any more smaller ones.'

'A stranger,' Abbott repeated, considering the proposition while he closed the door behind him. The boy's punctual arrival came as no surprise. From his window, and with wry amusement, he'd seen him walk past the hut several times, back and forth, his mouth moving as he counted his steps before he plumped himself down on the bottom step and stuck his bare legs straight out in front. The same as the previous day. Abbott saw the scabs on his knees and the scuffed shins. Pockets bulging with things he'd found and stored. Thick, wind-tossed curly hair. The tanned skinny arms and legs of a child who spent time outdoors rather than in front of a screen. For a while he watched the boy scoop and sift the sand, picking things out, then saw the snail shape emerge. Looking up occasionally and watching the boy's progress, Abbott sensed that when absorbed in these self-imposed challenges, the rest of the world vanished. Yes, even a man in a beach hut whom he wanted to talk to and be his friend. The boy had incredible powers of concentration.

'Because Mum says I mustn't talk to strangers.'

'Quite right.'

His open book of a face snapped shut and his shoulders drooped.

'But I'm not a stranger because you know where I live and we've already met and we've been for walks together and we've talked quite a bit,' Abbott continued. 'What do you think?'

'I think not.' With his head on one side, he looked hard at the man's face. So often he had to guess what grown-ups were thinking and he made mistakes. Like saying Hello to the couple who didn't like him. It had slipped out on a wave of worry and afterwards he had bitten his lip hard. 'So can we go for a walk together?' He ventured, curling back into himself ready for the blow.

'Why not. To the cove and back? Same as yesterday?'

His face cleared. Storm clouds of worry blew away. Joy and eagerness were as visible as if they had been written in letters on his forehead. And Abbott wondered what kind of a life this child led when an hour's company on a walk along a flat, featureless beach elicited such strong pleasure.

Before they set off, the boy bounded up the steps and slipped his small hand into the man's big one. Abbott let it rest there. The gesture spoke of trust and Abbott offered his acceptance. How could he betray it?

Down on the sand, Abbott looked steadfastly ahead but the boy glanced right and saw the tableau of two people in motion, getting ready to sign off for the day, and saw it freeze. Two people twisted their necks their way.

'They've seen us. They're watching us.'

'Fine. Doesn't matter. Ignore them. What we do is nothing to do with them.'

They walked on in silence but the boy's hand tightened.

'Maybe they'll tell people.'

'So what?'

'Well…Mum says I'm to go for a walk and then eat my chips. I'm not to bother anyone. I don't know if I'm allowed to be friends with you.'

And there it was. Out of the mouths of babes. While they walked on, straight down to the shore, Abbott struggled with the possibility that his support for this boy, however brief and casual and inconsequential, could backfire. For both of them. Two monologues vied for accuracy and authenticity.

This boy and I go for a walk together at five o'clock. It's my habit. It's his solitary routine. We coincided. We keep each other company. Why not? End of story. So just make sure you protect yourself and establish firm barriers and no harm can come of it. Even the most vicious of gossips can't create a scandal from a man and a boy going for an hour's walk in full view of every man, woman and child on the beach and promenade.

I've taken the first step into a personal mine field. The last thing I need right now is to be seen with a boy. A vulnerable boy.

A real worried voice interrupted. 'You see... they know I'm always by myself and they know there was no-one in the red hut 'til you came. They know everything.'

'So? You've met me now. What's wrong with that?'

'But I don't *know* you.'

'Look, stop worrying about those nosy people. They won't be here much longer.' *And nor will I and things will go back to how they were.* 'And I've already told them I know you and am happy to go for a walk with you.'

'Why?'

'Look, it's just to stop them bothering you. So they'll leave you alone.'

The boy inhaled sharply. 'But that's not true. You don't know me very well.' He sighed. 'And I'm not your friend yet. I'd like to be.'

'Then let's say we are friends, OK? Let's go for a walk, like we've done already, the last couple of days at five o'clock…'

'Ten past five.'

'…at ten past five and they'll see us and if they say anything I'll tell them I've been down here and lived in the hut before and I knew you then and we've met up again. Simple.'

'That's not true either.'

Abbott sighed. Why was this kid so sharp and honest? Others his age would take the plan for granted, even if it contained a small lie. They would shrug it into triviality. It *was* trivial. But Abbott sensed a layer of fear under the boy's skin, making him clear-sighted and wary. He had an uncanny wisdom. Perhaps it was this young kid's untarnished integrity that made it impossible to turn his back on him and throw out their walks and their conversations.

And let Daily Mail Man report him to Social Services? Nope. Can't be done. He had to answer the boy's clarity with his own honesty. How could he crush him?

'Let's put it this way. I'm getting to know you. We're getting to know each other. OK?'

The boy hesitated. 'OK.'

'Let's go. Before the rain comes.'

'I don't mind rain.'

'Me neither. Not a shower. But the wind's picked up a lot and that sky looks ready to open. I reckon we're in for a downfall.'

Neville turned his face to the sky. 'You don't know

with rain. Sometimes the clouds blow it away and sometimes it falls hard and sudden and bounces on top of the sea. I love that.'

'That belly load up there looks like serious rain to me.'

'Serious rain.' The words made him smile.

'Look at those crazy waves bashing each other about.'

'Yup. But I don't mind.'

I want to walk with you and talk to you even if we're caught in a massive storm.

'OK…we'll give it a go. Might have to turn back.'

'OK.'

A man and a boy, holding hands, set off as if in tracks, down to the shore before veering left and walking on the damp hard-packed surface just far enough away from the now troubled sea to avoid getting their feet wet. Even here, the wind was whipping away the sand and both of them lifted their free hands to wipe their eyes.

'So what do you do if the weather gets really bad? You don't stay out?'

'Sometimes I *have* to go home. If my clothes get really wet. Mum and I have a code for knocks on the door. I do two very loud and two not so loud and she comes and opens it as soon as she can.'

'I see.' He imagined a boy with dripping hair and a wet face and shorts stuck to bare legs standing in a gale on a doorstep, waiting to be let in by a woman whose hands are fully occupied with a client.

'Can we stop opposite the green boat?' the boy asked, changing the subject abruptly, as if wanting to let all of that go because it troubled him 'I always stop there.'

'OK.'

'I like to count the ups and downs.'

'Ups and downs?'

'As the boat rises and falls.'

Something lifted, maybe a tacit agreement to carry on in the present and not worry about the rest. The boy squeezed Abbott's hand more tightly. On they went, big strides matched by small catching-up ones as they continued on for a few yards until the boy came to a definite halt.

'Here,' he said, placing his feet together and turning to face the sea.

'Bit hard to see today.'

'I know. They all look nearly black. But that's the green one.' He pointed.

'Why do you like that one?'

'It's always alone. I keep it company.'

The boat rose and fell, tugging hard on its anchor chain. Most children punctuated silence with chatter, but this boy was content to watch and say nothing. He was comfortable. Abbott saw his mouth working and knew he was counting.

'A bigger number than usual,' he said finally.

'It's the wind getting up.'

'I know. Slow on a calm day and fast on a stormy one.'

Then with one of his sudden earnest shifts, 'I wish I could live on a boat.'

'Why?'

'Because it would be mine.' There was no need for further explanation.

'I've lived on a boat. Just for a short time,' Abbott said, wanting to share his love of the sea and his time on it.

'Oh.' Grey eyes unblinking.

'I sailed up the west coast of Scotland with a friend for two weeks. Do you know where that is?'

'Yes. I like looking at maps.' A new note of admiration coloured his voice and he squeezed the man's hand in little energetic bursts of enthusiasm. 'Wow! What was it like?'

'Very beautiful weaving in and out of the islands. Like being afloat on a private sea. We didn't see many other boats. It was very cold, often stormy, sometimes wet and misty, but always wonderful.'

'Were there beaches?'

'Everywhere. We sailed in and out of tiny hidden bays with white sand and craggy mountains behind. It's a wild landscape up there.'

'Were there rocks?'

'Many, many rocks to hurt a small sailing boat but they were all marked on the charts so we could be very careful and navigate round them.'

'Chart?'

'Like a map. A map of the sea and coast line with rocks and sunken boats marked on it so we know where to look out for danger.'

'Did you ever drop your anchor in a bay like this one? Same as the green boat?'

'No. We wanted to be alone so we dropped the anchor in remote places where we had the whole bay and the whole beach to ourselves. In the morning we would wake up to silence and seals flopped on rocks and no people.'

'Wow! I want to do that.'

'Maybe you will one day.'

'I've never been in a boat. I want to. I wish I could.'

'Never been in a rowing boat or a dinghy?'

'Nope.'

No, don't even think about the dinghy. Don't mention it. He doesn't know.

'Sometimes I sit in that boat at the end of the row of huts. I find two big sticks for oars and I put them in the… those…'

'Rowlocks.'

'Rowlocks and I pretend I'm on the sea. I wish I could really ride in it. Do you know who it belongs to?'

Damn. But no good lying.

'Yes. It's mine.'

'Yours? Wow!'

Abbott saw the small face light up with excitement, but saw too the holding back. The boy would not push his luck.

'I love that boat,' he allowed himself.

They stared out to sea.

'Was your boat much bigger? The one you sailed in?'

'Yes, of course. That's just a dinghy for pottering.'

The boy bit back his burning question. He knew not to pester the man.

'Did you have bunks in a cabin?' After a long pause. Like he was preoccupied and longed to twist the conversation back the other way.

'Of course. You need shelter after you've been standing on deck all day. Somewhere dry and warm… because it rained a lot and we got cold. The cabin was snug.' Abbott was aware he was rabbiting on to distract the boy from a different possibility.

'Like the hut.'

'Very like the hut. Except the boat rocked gently all the time on the waves.'

As if a sign had been exchanged, both turned from the green boat at the same moment and walked on. Clouds dashed across a fast darkening sky and squalls raced over the surface of the sea and beat it into confusion. They could both smell the advancing rain.

The first big drops fell, staining the sand around their feet the colour of cement. Abbott looked up at the wind-strewn sky but the boy didn't seem to notice, perhaps lost in thoughts of boats big and small. As the lid of the sky came down, the sand lost its already muted colour and turned grey. An invisible sun, its rays extinguished, slipped towards the horizon behind a mountain of storm clouds. From one end of the bay to the other, and far out to sea, white-tipped waves jostled and bumped together, like people rushing in a crowd or on a station platform. At the shore's edge, the sea's energy quickened. Of course, it had to happen. The next wave was a wild card that threw itself right up the beach and caught them in a race of frothing water that exploded over their feet.

The boy laughed, looked down, then up. 'My feet are wet.'

'Mine too.'

Two pairs of shoes were instantly soaked. Two faces crumpled with laughter.

'The green boat is going crazy.'

'I can see.'

'I hope it doesn't break its chain. A boat did that once and got carried along the shore really fast and ended up on the rocks all broken and splintered. I found bits of it on the sand and in the pools the next day. Lots of pieces of wood. Pans and the steering wheel and a fire extinguisher. Some shoes. And I peeped into the cabin because the roof was torn off. The seats and beds were all torn and soaked. Ruined.' He shrugged his shoulders as if hurt by the memory.

'What happened to it?'

'Oh the owners came but it was too badly broken to be mended.' He sighed. 'A crane took it away and the local people cleared up the rest of the stuff.'

'That's sad.'

'I know.'

Another surging wave bounced in and swirled up to their ankles. Caught by the emotion of the boy's story-telling, Abbott had stopped watching. 'We'd better go,' he said. 'We can't walk with shoes full of water.'

'Where?' The disappointment was palpable. 'I don't mind being wet.'

'I do. These are the only shoes I have.'

'It's not time for me to go home yet.'

Oh heavens.

'Look, how about this for a plan. We'll slosh back up the beach before the heavens open and get your chips and you can eat them in my hut instead of getting even wetter on the wall.'

'But I can sit in the bus shelter...' And the sub-text, loud and clear, was *But I'd love not to*. Again the boy didn't push his luck as others would have done.

Abbott couldn't take advantage of such honesty. 'Come on! Run!' he shouted, knowing as soon as the word was out that running was the last thing they could do. Bent against the strong wind, and with wet shoes that gathered great clods of sand on the soles, they could barely walk. Alone, Abbott might have managed a plodding sprint but with a small boy at his side, clinging to his hand, it took much longer. Why didn't he think to just take off their shoes? On they squelched and of course the heavens *did* open and dumped a sky-full of water right on top of them.

What do we look like? A large man in a ridiculous weighed-down coat with a small boy leaping and laughing

142

at his side high-stepping through torrential rain?

'Now that's what I call wet,' the chip man said with a grin. 'Better run home, son, and change those clothes before you catch your death of cold.' Perhaps he hadn't noticed that the two of them were together. He, too, had been sheltering from the rain, hunkered down inside his kiosk. He hadn't expected any customers.

'It's not time to go home yet.' Again, the honesty.

'Not even when it's this wet?'

'Nope.'

'He's going to eat his chips in my hut and dry off a bit. Two cones please. Extra large.' Abbott handed over a fiver. 'Keep the change, mate.'

Neville's wide grin broke like sunshine. Then faded into a frown. 'The chips will get wet.'

'I'll tuck them inside my coat.' *Where they'll leave dark stains of chip fat.*

'OK. But your coat will be stinky.'

'Better than wet chips.'

The boy grinned and hopped from one heavy foot to the other. Abbott stowed the chips inside his coat and covered them with his lapel. Off they went, holding hands, smelling of vinegar, and laughing at the rain that battered their faces. The chip man watched them and felt chuffed that the kid had finally found someone to take care of him. Nice bloke.

15
Day 6

THEY WALKED DOWN the concrete steps, their heads down, bodies hunched, through punishingly hard rain. A child would have drawn it as straight black lines falling from a heavily scribbled charcoal sky. Impervious, perhaps almost oblivious, the boy bounced along at the man's side, fizzing with anticipation and joy, glancing up every few paces to make sure that this was for real. Water ran down his face from his soaked hair and he kept blinking it out of his eyes. Abbott saw the long, glistening eyelashes. The anorak was almost certainly not waterproof and the cotton shorts would have to be wrung out. There was so much wet sand stuck to his jelly shoes that they must have weighed a ton but he ploughed on regardless, lifting his legs very high with every step, offering not one word of complaint.

Inside Abbott's coat, tucked behind his out-turned lapels, the two cardboard cones of chips leaked warmth and sogginess. *Shakespearean weather,* he thought as they trudged on. *Lear and his fool.*

On the verandah they shook themselves like dogs.

'Take off your clothes here or we'll make everywhere wet,' Abbott said.

'All of them?' *He must be joking.*

'No, silly, just the outer layers. Here, kick off those ridiculous sandals. Take off your anorak and shorts and just leave them here in a pile by the door. I'll deal with them in a minute. Let's get you inside and dry first.'

While the boy struggled to peel off wet, skin-clinging clothes, Abbott threw off his cap, trod out of his gritty wet trainers and shrugged himself out of a woollen coat that was heavy and dense with water. Like a drenched animal. But first he rescued the two packets of chips and pulled the key from his trouser pocket.

'OK, quick! In you go! And stand inside the door while I find towels. Don't move!'

There was no need to tell the boy to stand still. The rain forgotten, his damp body of no consequence even while it dripped a puddle around his feet, he stared round and breathed his astonishment and contentment. His utter delight. With night closing in early, and the thunder clouds shutting off any remaining evening light, it was almost dark inside. Yet, as his eyes adjusted, he drank it in; the high bed, the gauze curtains, the books, the colour red.

The hut was everything he had dreamed of – like the inside of a boat or a caravan or a magic cave. If he could choose where he would live for ever and ever, it would be here.

'You OK there for a few minutes? Just hang on!' Abbott called and received a rapturous nod. There were things to sort and he didn't want the boy wandering off and dripping water on the bedding and books. The cones of chips were deposited on the kitchen work surface. Then he found his biggest white towel and came back to rub the boy's hair until it stood in peaks before wrapping him up in it and tucking the ends in so the whole small body was encased and warm.

'Don't move!' There was teasing in his voice, and in his soul an unbidden satisfaction and sympathy when he stopped for a second and took in the sight of the swaddled child, leaning with glowing contentment against the door. Grabbing another towel, he rubbed his own head before climbing out of his wet jeans and into his spare ones and swapping the wet t-shirt for a dry one. He dried his feet, not wanting to tread more water and sand across the floor. He was conscious of the boy's eyes on him, but nothing was said. *Ah... he doesn't have a father. Maybe he's never seen a man stripping off.* The thought came and vanished as he concentrated on the practical.

'Budge!' He was by the boy again, opening the door for a second and throwing his own wet clothes onto the heap outside. If the rain cleared, his clothes would dry in the wind tomorrow, though his coat might be doomed. Later. He would work it out later.

And still the boy looked on with an expression of trust. Still and silent.

Fascinated and satisfied by every move the man made, each one careful and sure and quiet, the boy observed and said nothing. He was like someone in the audience of an entrancing play or at a concert of heart-stopping music, not wanting to cough or make a sound in case it broke the spell. It took the physical effort of biting his lips to hold in the questions and his wish to say Thank you to the kind man.

Abbott took the cover from the oil lamp, struck a match and waited for the flame to fly round the wick before replacing the glass dome. Neville watched the flickering pale flame grow into a leaping yellow flare that filled the room, covering everything with warm colour.

That's why the light had come on gradually the other night. It wasn't a switch for an electric light, it was a lamp. This oil lamp.

'Right… better close the blind… and the curtains…' Abbott said, talking to himself and reaching up above the table, 'then you're allowed to move and we'll have a drink and eat our chips.' He winked at the boy.

'I don't mind not moving.'

Abbott heard the undertow of gratitude and a boy's excitement at a wet evening that had turned into an adventure.

But from his own perspective? And seen through someone else's eyes? Here in his hut was a half-naked, perhaps vulnerable boy wrapped in a towel. Wouldn't look too good.

But who's looking? And it can't be helped. The boy could hardly trudge home in that state. It would have been cruel. He'll go soon. No harm done.

Another voice answered the first.

You should have sent him home with his wet chips in his wet clothes. Must have happened before. What the hell are you playing at, Abbott? Like you just have to go further into the fucking mess you've already created. You got a death wish, or what?

And the repeated reply.

No-one's looking.

He shoved the warring voices to the back burner at the same time as he shut out the world.

'OK, we're hidden. Go and sit on the floor with your back against the bookcase,' he said. 'Pull a pillow off the bed and make yourself comfortable. Are you drying out?'

'Yes.' The answer was automatic. He hadn't given it a thought. Didn't matter. He did as he was told, propped himself up and was soon facing the other way, taking in more and more of the hut's wondrous interior as the man moved around the tiny kitchen, getting out a pan, pouring water from a big bottle, lighting the gas.

'Tea or red wine?' he asked, filling a purple glass to the brim.

The boy glanced up. 'Tea. I don't drink wine.' Then he caught the man's eye and grinned.

'You will one day.' He winked. 'Tea tonight then. Milk and sugar?'

'Yes.' He eyed the two cones of chips still on the counter.

Bet they're getting cold, but it doesn't matter.

In three and a half minutes – the boy was counting and checking his counting against his watch – the man was beside him, handing down a mug of tea and a fat cone of chips.

'OK?'

Neville nodded. *More than OK.*

After returning to get his own chips and glass of wine, Abbott folded his large frame and sat on the floor too, his long legs stretching way out into the room. The boy was still huddled in his towel, knees drawn up to his chin, but he'd freed his arms and hands to raise and lower the mug and to poke chips into his mouth. Abbott glanced at the top of his skinny white chest and the sharp-carved collar bones. The boy's thin arms. So close up, he saw for the first time the beauty of the boy's symmetrical face with its confetti covering of freckles on his nose and cheek bones. His skin was tanned from all the beach walks. His eyes were the grey of smoke and rain and English landscapes.

This boyish prettiness won't last much longer but he'll grow into a gorgeous youth. A simple assessment with no hidden meaning or longing.

'They're not wet,' said the boy, appreciative, chewing.

'Nope. The chips survived. How about you?'

'I'm fine.'

And so, unexpectedly, was Abbott. Eating chips on the floor next to a boy who exuded happiness was relaxing and heart-warming. Maybe he'd had too much of his own company, though it had been only four or five days on his own. He'd lost count. Or maybe he felt a kinship with this boy who was not one of the gang and who, like him, preferred to live his life out of view of others. He lifted a greasy finger and stroked the boy's face. It was a simple gesture of affection, a substitute for words, like 'You're a good kid' or 'I like your company' or just 'You're safe with me.'

Safe. The word hovered and twisted into a lie. Others, in his place, here beside a damp half-naked child, might have used the same word. *You're safe. Safe with me. I won't hurt you.* Others, the twisted, sick ones with whom he might have already been lumped, might have unwrapped the towel and stroked the young male body, ignoring the surprise and concern and discomfort as stroking became kissing and kisses became aggressive and moved from chest to face, a tongue pushed between virgin lips. Then forced, painful sex which would hurt and crush a child and turn trust to terror. Others, those who were now being rooted out from the grotesquely corrupt corridors of power in almost every institution in the land, could break this child as easily as stamping on a dragonfly and disabling its wings so that it would never fly again. Here. Now. It was unthinkable, yet the thought took shape because he knew how much cruelty had already been inflicted on boys just like this one who sat beside him, his trust intact.

Reaching out, he put an arm round the skinny shoulders that were now warm and relaxed under the towel. The boy leant in, tucking his head on Abbott's shoulder, a smile curling around each chunky chip. They ate and sipped. The silence told Abbott that the boy had stopped counting. The two cuddled close until the cones were empty, then they sat some more in comfortable silence broken by small content shivers and sighs.

'I wish I lived here.' The words escaped even though he had tried hard to hold them inside.

'But it's only a beach hut. Even I don't really live here.' His tone was casual but he knew he was answering honesty with dismissal.

'I'd still like to.' A long silence. Dare he say it? 'I'd like to live here with you.'

'Well, there isn't room for two of us and you have

your own home. And your mum.'

Heavens, Abbott, how can you give him bland nothings when the boy is risking so much?

'I wish you were my dad.' The boy said the words very quietly before turning his head away, knowing this was too much.

Abbott said nothing. The boy heard the full stop at the end of his last sentence. For a while they sat in silence, waiting for the curtain to fall on an intimacy that had gone a few words too far.

'I can't go home in this towel.' A rapid, face-saving change of subject which both of them heard and acknowledged. And anyway, the boy's internal clock was ticking louder now and he knew he couldn't prolong his time in the warmth of the man's hut, nor in the sweet feel of the man's presence next to him.

'Nope. Sorry. That would look pretty daft.' Abbott sighed, withdrew his arm and peeled away. He rose and peeped out of the window. 'It's not raining nearly so hard now. The worst is over.'

'So what do I wear?'

'Well…the same clothes you came in.'

'They're wet.'

'I know… I'm sorry… but you'll just have to put them back on.' *What other solution is there?*

'Thought so. And walk. 'Cause you don't have a car.'

'Nope. No car.'

'I'm already seven minutes late.'

They were both back on track. The temperature of their relationship was muted and manageable again. The thermostat had corrected itself.

He offered not a word of complaint. The boy was up, towel abandoned on the floor and heading out of the door in his t-shirt and pants, thin legs two-tone, white and brown where his shorts cut off the sunburn. In the darkness outside, Abbott could see the jerky movements of a small figure fighting his way into wet shorts that stuck to his skin. Then he was off, down the steps, one arm pushing through the sleeve of his anorak, carrying sand-encrusted jelly shoes in the other hand. Once again, Abbott was taken aback by the boy's acceptance of what had to be. No fuss. No drama.

Half way along the beach, Neville stopped and turned. There was a single wave and then he was running hard, perhaps to shorten the seven minutes to six or five.

16
Day 6

S HARON HAD BEEN on lookout duty since her last client had left early at six on the dot, not wanting his usual long, mind-numbingly tedious session. While servicing the bloke, she'd glanced often at the threatening clouds and fast darkening sky through the bedroom window and hoped Neville would have the sense to head home. While her hands did the work, she detached herself and thought about other things, like what she needed from Tesco and what would happen next on Hollyoaks. She had to absent herself or the work would be insufferable and destructive. The first drops of rain against glass were as hard as bullets, heard first, then seen. Bullets became steady gunfire. Rain drummed against all the windows, drowning out the man's murmurs and moans. Maybe it was the noise which distracted him and caused his enthusiasm and erection to wither. Fine by her that he lost interest, got up, zipped up his flies and sauntered out of the room. There were no words, no eye contact, just a brief handshake and the exchange of fivers which she counted quickly while she walked him to the door. It was a commercial transaction and he'd paid her the full whack. Fine. He was a regular and would be back. God, men and their bloody dicks. She kicked off her heels, went into the bathroom to wash her hands and coat them with anti-bacterial gel before getting into the shower and washing away the day's work. Dropping the circus outfit in the washing basket, she pulled on her jeans and an old t-shirt and worried some more about where Neville had got to.

The man gone, the bedroom very quickly restored to domesticity, she paced the living room, stopping to peer out at the murk and to see if a small wet figure was making his way along the street. Worry grew to concern and guilt. Always the guilt.

There he was. Finally she spotted him and had the door open and ready, even though the wind blew the rain straight in.

'You're soaked to the skin, son!'

'It's raining…'

'I know it's bloody raining! I've been worried about you. Why didn't you come home?'

'I was OK.'

'You couldn't be OK in that. It's really heavy rain. And

you're late.' She tried to keep the anger and worry out of her voice. After all, whose fault was it really?

'Only six minutes.'

'Oh son…' She pushed the door shut behind him and bent to hug his wet body. 'You're bloody sodden. Come on, let's get you out of these clothes.'

The second time today.

Neville obediently lifted one leg, then the other, while his mum pulled off the jelly sandals, clean again now from walking back through deep puddles and rivers of rain in gutters. He stood still while she tugged down shorts that clung like a second skin to his legs. He stuck out his arms so she could free him of the anorak and the sodden t-shirt. *Like a puppet,* he thought.

'Fat lot of good that anorak did. You need a new one. Look, I'll run you a bath. You're wet through. Come on… let's get you warmed up.'

While she ran the water, he stepped out of his pants and shivered. Until then, he hadn't noticed how cold he was from the second soaking during his dash home.

'Right…in you get and stay there until you're really warm. I'll get you something to eat. I don't suppose you managed to get your chips.'

'I did.'

'Oh heavens… in this? Where did you eat them?'

Neville paused. 'In the bus shelter.' He said a silent *Sorry* because it was a lie.

In the bath, Neville thought about counting stars and counting grains of sand and his mind went back to the red hut where he was wrapped in a big white towel, eating chips, and talking to a man who was his friend. Searching for the right words, he found *kind* and *trusting*. If he had been older, he might have told himself that the man treated him almost as an equal, without patronising him, without laughing at him.

'Wherever were you?' Sharon asked, sliding a plate of spaghetti hoops across the small formica table, then buttering sliced white bread for both of them, eating hers with a mug of warm white wine.

'Same as always. On the beach. Then when it rained I went and sat in the bus shelter. I said.'

Sharon shook her head. 'Why didn't you come back?'

'You said stay out 'til half past six.' A fair enough reason.

'I know, son, but not in this weather. You know that.'

The spaghetti hoops were hot but nothing like as good as the chips. 'You said sit in the bus shelter if it rains.'

Oh god, he was so damn literal. 'If you remember, I said sit in the bus shelter if it rains a bit but I don't expect you to walk about in a storm.'

'It wasn't a storm.'

'It was bloody heavy rain. Look, you know what I mean.'

'But the men would still be here.'

'So what? Doesn't matter.'

It was all so confusing. Why couldn't she stick to the rules? He understood rules.

'I mustn't come home until the men have gone.'

Dumping her fork on her plate, she took his sauce-smeared face in her hands and spoke through threatening tears. 'Look, if it's too cold or too wet or you're not happy, you come home. You matter much more than my clients. I can let you in and you can go into your room. I know I said stay out but that was when it was summer.'

'It rains in summer.'

'Neville, I know! You're not listening. Stop blocking me off.'

Oh but he *was* listening and trying to piece together the new rules which slid about and wouldn't drop into a definite shape. Things had to be the same. *Constant.* And under the worry about rules was the stronger worry that she would find out where he had really been and would stop him going there again.

Don't tell. Don't let any words slip out. The secret belongs to me and the man…Abbott.

Sharon watched the worry lines cross and crease her son's face. Like her, he had stopped eating. 'Eat your supper. You need something warm in you.'

'I had chips.'

'I know you had chips.' She pictured him in a dripping bus shelter pulling wet bits of potato out of a wet cardboard cone and again fought back the tears. He hated to see her upset. 'OK, I know you like everything to be very clear so I'll say it again. Now it's nearly autumn you're to come back if it's too cold or too wet to walk on the beach.'

He nodded.

Or I could go to the red hut where I'm not cold or wet.

'And when the weather gets really bad, you'll stay here in your room. OK?'

But I hate staying in my room for a long long time with weird noises coming from my mum's room. Like being put in a cage. I'd rather walk on the beach.

'I don't like that.'

'It's not perfect, I know, but I'll buy you some new books and you can do some colouring.' Through her false cheeriness she heard a voice that would sooth a much younger child. Not her son. Heavens, he was fast approaching an age where being in the house when she had clients would be impossible. Very soon, any day now, he would start to understand, and then she would have to think again. Hard.

'Maybe I can get you your own TV.'

Yup, great idea, Sharon! Except you don't have a bean to pay for one let alone the licence. And it won't exactly solve the problem. It's looking like you're going to have to find somewhere else to work. A seedy hotel room. Fuck!

For a moment he brightened. 'I'd still rather go out than stay in my room. Even with a TV.'

'I know. You said. What's so bad about your room?'

'I don't want men coming in.'

'Of course not. None would. Why do you say that?'

'One did once.' He put another spoonful of now cold orange pasta into his mouth and looked up at her. 'That day that man shouted at you.'

Loads of men shout at me.

'Which man?'

'When I had the flu.'

Yeah, I think I remember. But that was months ago, soon after I started working on my own, and we talked about it after. Not a lot. The kid's said nothing else until now. The police had caught the two of us, Janie and me, working together and looking out for one another and said we were running a brothel. Fucking stupid police rule. One sex worker's earning a bit on the side. Two's a brothel. So now I'm classed as a single girl who charges for sex and that's allowed so long as I don't walk the streets. I work by myself and sometimes I get beaten up. The police are fine with that.

'I think I know who you mean, son. It was nothing. Don't worry about it.'

'Wasn't nothing.'

He'd stopped eating again and was looking deep into her eyes, sussing out the truth. And she hadn't given it to him.

'OK, let's talk about it again. Maybe I can reassure you.'

'Reassure?'

'Make it better. Better talk about it if it's worrying you.'

'What for? You already know. You did talk to me.'

Yeah but perhaps not enough.

She never had enough time for the boy. She sighed and reached out to take his hand in hers. 'I don't always know what goes on in your head. I don't know if we remember things the same way. OK? So how about you tell me again.'

'It was a Tuesday and he was the second man.'

'OK.'

'And I wasn't well and you said to stay in my room and not go to the beach.'

She thought she could recall the evening he meant, but she'd learnt to erase her clients because then they couldn't get to her. Wipe it all clean at the end of each evening – her room, her body and her head.

'So what do you remember, son?'

'A man shouted a lot and you shouted and then you were crying.'

It flashed back. Oh my god, yes. That sodding tosser of a client. Not one of her regulars, in fact she'd never seen him before or since. Maybe a travelling salesman. Or a tourist. If they told her about themselves, fine, and some poor sods *only* wanted to talk because they were lonely and came because she listened, but she never asked questions. Yeah, some men got angry and aggressive when they couldn't get a hard on and blamed her instead of themselves. If things started to get out of hand and she sensed danger, she'd stop and tell the man to go without charging him. She could handle it. She had no choice. Other women took the same risks because they too had no choice and a few had taken a battering. How to explain that to her son?

'I remember now. He was drunk and in a bad temper. I threw him out and he wasn't happy about it. He made a lot of noise, that's all. I thought you were OK about it.'

'No. No. No. I heard the man shouting and then I heard you screaming so I came out of my room to help you and opened your door and saw he had hold of your arm and was twisting it behind your back and he was hurting you and tearing your sparkly top only he saw me looking in and he swore a lot of bad words and let go of you and you yelled at him GET OUT OF THIS HOUSE and went back into your room and you started to take off your torn clothes and another man who'd been waiting in the living room went into your bedroom and was nice to you and put his arm round you and I heard him say It's OK, love. It's OK. And then he closed the bedroom door and it was quiet after that.'

Sharon's tired face was ashen. For a few heartbeats she couldn't speak. 'But that was the end of it. And it didn't happen again,' she said, her voice tear-filled and tentative. It had happened again, but not when he was here.

'No. Just once.'

'OK, you must forget about it now. No-one's going to

hurt me. It won't happen again.' *Lies.*

'I don't know that.'

'You have to believe me.' *More lies.*

Her son was frowning and tears filled his eyes. He looked up at her. 'But I can't forget it because he was horrid to me too.'

What? For god's sake, now what? So far he had been accurate to the last detail but this was something new. And, she prayed, imagined. Invented.

'He was horrid to you? What do you mean?' Sharon's eyes were wide with dread.

Neville hung his head. He had meant to keep it a secret, not wanting to upset his mum any further.

'What, son? Tell me.' Her grip on his hand tightened.

'Well... he didn't actually leave the house straightaway. He came into my room first and said bad things and hurt me.'

'No, son. He left.' Her heart was pounding but she tried to keep the panic out of her voice, tried to think back and gather up the memory in the short empty space before he spoke again. She'd seen him out, hadn't she? *Thrown* him out.

'You *told* him to get out but the other man went in and comforted you so you didn't see.'

'And...'

'He came into my room and said if I ever told anyone he would come back and hurt you properly and he'd hurt me too.' In his head he started counting the spaghetti hoops left on his plate because it was too hard to say the next bit. Seven, eight, nine… His mum looked like a china doll, like the one in the antiques shop in town with wide-open eyes that didn't blink and skin that was as white as flour. Her mascara was running a bit after she'd stood at the stove. She had more hoops left than him. Twelve, thirteen, fourteen…

'Go on, Neville.' She forced herself to stay calm.

'You've got seventeen hoops left.'

'I said, go on.'

He took a deep breath and made a huge effort not to count. 'He was strong and he threw me on the bed and held me down and said horrible things but in a quiet voice so you wouldn't hear and…'

'And then he left?'

'No.' He waited. 'No. He pulled down my shorts and laughed at me.'

Christ. Jesus fucking christ. He wouldn't make this up. Couldn't.

'He did what? Tell me. Exactly.'

'He laughed at me. He pointed at my willy and laughed.' Seeing his mother's eyes flood and spill with tears, he added quickly, 'Only for a minute. Then he left. He didn't hurt me much.'

'Did he touch you?' Sharon held her breath.

'Yes, I said. He shoved me and held me down.'

'Did he touch you when he pulled down your shorts?'

Neville looked puzzled. 'Nope.'

'Not at all?'

'Nope.'

The long swollen silence was broken by the quiet crying of a child who had hurt his mother and the violent, heaving sobs of a mother who had betrayed her child. In a choreographed move, both got down from the table and clung to each other. Neville counted the seconds then the minutes that they stood like statues glued together until his mum peeled herself away, sat on a chair and pulled him to her, still holding his hands in hers.

'I'm so sorry. Words don't help you much, I know, but I'm so terribly sorry. I had no idea. Why didn't you tell me before?'

But she knew why and knew this was a futile line of argument. She'd read that children who were regularly abused stayed silent for years. Even decades. It was all over the news. But this had happened just once, and he'd not actually been abused, and he'd managed to tell her. Thank god. She let her question go. 'OK, I understand why it was hard to tell me. You've done really well to tell me now. Maybe tomorrow I'll phone the police and tell them what he did. They may want you to describe him…say what he looked like. Do you think you can do that?'

'I don't know.'

'You saw his face.'

'I closed my eyes.'

Sharon sighed.

As if the police would take a blind bit of notice. Even if I told them one of my clients is one of their own top brass. Kinky bastard. They'd say, 'Don't threaten us, darling. So a punter shouted at your son. Sure you want to report it? Sure you want us to get out the At Risk register again? Social workers at your door, packing him like lost luggage in a bag? You want that? I didn't think so.'

She returned to the present and looked her son up and down as if searching for damage now, long after the event. 'Let's get you to bed.'

'OK.'

'And tomorrow I'll cancel my clients and be with you in the evening.'

'No.' Sharp and insistent.

'What?'

'I'd rather go for a walk. Like I always do.'

And because she understood that his routine was more important than anything else and that to change it would be upsetting and disruptive for him, she consented. After all, he was safer on the bloody beach than in his own house.

17
Day 7

*L*IKE WAKING UP *inside a chrysalis,* he thought, when he opened his eyes the next morning to soft red light twice filtered through the smoke-screen curtains over the window and the one pulled across the length of his bed. Like a child had coloured the whole room with a large waxy crayon. The walls were deep pink. The silver of the cafetière, left on the table, shone with streaks of claret. For a while the previous evening was lost in the remnants of dreams, and then he remembered the wet chips and smiled and wondered if the boy had got himself home safely. And if he'd got a row for being six or seven minutes late. If he'd caught a chill. Well, he'd find out because he'd be outside the hut again at ten past five. Abbott smiled.

Stretching his arms behind him, he lay for a long time listening to the sea on its unstoppable journey up the beach and to the morning call of birds winging over the water. The hammer blows of shock that had been hitting him each time he emerged from sleep were muted to a mild anxiety. The adrenalin of fear had slowed in his veins. The panic of his situation had ebbed away so quickly, like the tide, leaving resignation and stasis. His need to go over and over the story was extinguished because he knew it by heart and there was no more to say. Fragments still surfaced, unexpectedly, but he could exert mental muscle and push them back down. Like shoving and holding something under water. He thanked the sea, the silence, the solitude and privacy, for bringing him a transient peace, broken less often by shock waves of what was to come. He recognised this pause for what it was, an interlude in a play whose second act would inevitably start up again, but he was not in a theatre and there was no bell to tell him to return to his seat and wait for the action.

Tesco ground coffee tasted like exclusive single estate in his sanctuary. He slid his hand over the white china mug, remembering the flimsy plastic beakers placed under a brown trickle from the drinks machine in his office. On a white plate, two slices of sourdough bread thickly spread with butter and apricot jam waited a first crunchy bite. Outside was the view of sand, more ochre than wet cement in this morning's weak but gilded sunlight. Beyond it rolled a slow-moving sea that demanded no response. In another life he would be answering an endless stream of insistent emails, banging on keys with one hand, holding the flimsy slopping cup with other, lifting it to his mouth for untasted gulps. In the next cubicle would be Jim, a mirror image, going through exactly the same actions. Type, gulp, react.

No screens. No mobile. No talking. Time. Endless time.

One goes on and on, running on the same treadmill, never considering an alternative until forced to stop, he thought.

But the other voice, Jim's, replied, *'Nah, you'll be bored in ten minutes, mate. You're good, one of the best. You can reach the most messed up, bottled-up lads where others fail. You can get under their skins and you don't threaten them. And I've watched you take pride in that.'*

Yes. True. *'But, Jim...maybe it's time to stop. It's been fifteen years. Even after paying the price – and it will be steep – there are other choices out there. It's only now that I can see them.*

After the lingered-over breakfast, he put things straight. Tidied the kitchen area. Smoothed his bed. This small space spoke to him of being ship-shape and indeed it had the feel of a cabin in a small sailing boat. And step by step he was claiming it as his own, confident enough now to put away more of his aunt's belongings, not that there were many, and to replace them with his own. How long, he wondered, would it feel a luxury to move at snail's pace and to run his fingers over the rough texture of the lump of driftwood that stood like a sentry by the door? From the table, he looked out at see-through clouds that moved like breath, changing shape as they crossed an anaemic blue sky. The washed-out colours of a very early English autumn. A memory followed. Just as slow and blurred. Then more defined. Then imperative. Abbott jumped up, rummaged behind the bed and extracted his rucksack, then the photograph.

It was monochrome in a plain black frame. A face too unusual to be conventionally handsome, the features large and sensual in the long face. Deeply set blue eyes gave little away. Long fair hair was roughly fingered back and damp because the man had been swimming. A long aquiline nose. Full, curved lips twisted into a wry, lop-sided smile as if to say, *Give over, go away! Fuck off!* And, *Yeah, I love you too.* Or did Abbott imagine that, reading what he wanted in the teasing, flirting expression?

It had been in another small house facing the sea, high on a cliff. The soundtracks they had listened to that evening, over and over, started up in his mind as if he'd pressed PLAY. *The Power of Love. How Deep Is Your Love.* Before he'd run away, he'd grabbed a pile of CDs of Celine Dion, Marvyn Gaye and Bob Marley and shoved them in his rucksack, but there was nothing to play them on. No laptop. No electricity. Damn. The falling apple moment came only after he'd made a second cafetière of coffee and was sitting staring into space. *Idiot!* He swatted his forehead at his own stupidity. Surely somewhere sells old-fashioned CD players in the town. And head-phones. Or ear buds. And batteries. His need to hear the songs again was urgent, the silence no longer sufficient nor bulwark enough against the past. An hour passed. He walked through the rooms of his memories, allowing himself to be moved almost to tears.

What's got into you? Brain-washed by the sea or what? You've left something out, Abbott. You've left out the ending of that story which along with your absurd neglect to log out on a secure website sent you scuttling here. Why are you telling yourself the sanitised version and pressing the pause button just before your lover led you by the hand to the screen and used your credit card and punched keys and showed you youths and boys doing what you and he had just done together? You watched, both high on alcohol and fucking. You kissed and fondled each other in front of the images. Until you came to your senses, realised the adolescents in the images didn't just look *young, they* were *young, and shut it down. You confronted him and he had laughed. You shouted. He shouted back. You told him to go. He mocked your uptight morals – what difference did a year or two make? – shrugged on his clothes and walked. But it was five years ago, for fuck's sake. And up to the violent parting, it had all unrolled with more than willing consent on both sides. OK, Luke took advantage but there was no malice. No intent to hurt. Luke was after illicit pleasure, unaware that for Abbott it was a turn off and a no man's land. Let it go, Abbott! Let* him *go. It's history. Don't go there. Stay here in the hut where you can pretend to be safe.*

The volume on the remembered songs faded and finally died. As did the pulling back of the past to explain the present. He slid the photo back into the rucksack and stashed it behind the bed. He stood up, stretched and poked his head out of the hut. When he set off along the beach, he was no longer on red alert, but upset and angry with himself for coming up with such a load of bollocks. He sighed. Must be shock or something.

There were about a dozen couples on the beach, behind wind screens, still dressed but braving the cooler temperatures. And Them. The Vigilantes. The door of their hut was wide open. Table and chairs were out, coffee mugs in hands, tabloid newspaper and women's magazine held up but eyes darting away from pages in constant surveillance. A human scanning machine. *Damn them.* Having that pair so close seemed too cruel an irony. People without lives. Stirrers. Trouble. He set off, ostentatiously holding carrier bags, head down, very interested in the roughed up sand as if looking for something.

'Morning!'

It was like the fairy tale Billy Goats Gruff in which you had to get over the bridge trip-trap-trip-trap before the troll leapt out and got you. Abbott wasn't frightened of the troll who read The Mail and did Citizens' Look Out Duty, but he was irritated that he had to waste his energy on pointless exchanges and nosiness thinly disguised as conversation. And he was worried he would say something he'd regret. *Mask on,* he reminded himself. *Blank face. Bland words.*

'Good morning,' he replied with a nod, moving past as fast as he could without appearing rude. His sighs of exasperation went unheard. Just.

'Shocking weather yesterday afternoon.' Bill put down his Mail. 'That rain! Saw you got caught in it. Bet you got a skinful.'

So they had been watching.

'Were you with that boy? Hard to see in that downpour.'

Yeah, of course you could bloody see. And I can hear the edginess in your voice, like criticism, like a warning. Like, Look out, we're starting to draw a few conclusions here.

'Yeah. The rain was heavy.' Non-committal. Give nothing away.

'We was just packing up when the sky turned black. I said to Bill that we'd better get a move on before it dumped on us. It's not usually like that at this time of year. Not that kind of rain. Hope you and the boy got yourselves nice and dry in your hut.' Ida wasn't managing to hide her fascination. Her longing to know.

Don't give them a thing. She's fishing but she won't

catch anything. Not a minnow of information.

'This cool weather'll chase the tourists away.' Bill continued, throwing a warning glance at his wife as he deliberately changed tack. 'The forecast is for a fresher day tomorrow and maybe the next, but then more rain. Don't know when we'll get down tomorrow because we're making a formal complaint about that neighbour we told you about. All the council houses in our road are owner occupied. It's the only one still for rent and we want it put on the market. People who own their houses look after them and take care of them. We don't want someone put in there by the council.'

If Bill was waiting for a sympathetic response, none came.

Ida reverted to the weather but it was a pretext. 'Hope you've got plenty to occupy you 'cause you won't be getting out much over the next couple of days. Unless you like walking in the rain. I don't suppose you'll be taking that boy with you if it's really bad.'

Bloody cheek. It's none of your business what I do.

'Won't be long before the place is deserted.' The safe retreat again. Like they stuck in the poison dart then pulled it out again.

'I suppose so.' Abbott could barely bring himself to reply.

'Maybe the weather doesn't make much difference to you if you've got writing to keep you busy. How's it going then?' Terrier-like, Ida was not letting go.

Abbott had ground to a halt while shifting from one foot to the other, signalling his wish to get away without being downright rude. He stood there giving all the signals that he was a man in a hurry. Urgent shopping to be done.

'Well, thank you,' he muttered.

'That's good. It must be a bit lonely on your own.'

'No. I like it.' Through gritted teeth.

Can't you just leave me alone? Let me off your hook? Allow me to go shopping without further interrogation?

'Been meaning to ask you… we was just wondering… since you're around now and we saw you with him…'

Now what?

Her tone preempted something nasty in the woodshed and he guessed correctly before a word was out what it would be about.

'We wonder if you know about that boy who hangs about here every evening around five. Maybe he's not told you. Just a friendly warning.' She paused and looked straight at him. 'He's known around here. The other day when we was packing up he stopped and said Hello but we didn't want him bothering us. Bill told him to leave us alone. I think he went on to your hut.' She waited.

You know he went to my hut and you know we left together. You know we walked in the rain yesterday. But I'm not giving you the satisfaction of acknowledging it nor commenting on it. It's none of your bloody business.

'Then yesterday when it was raining cats and dogs there he was out in it but you took pity on him, didn't you?' Bill joined in. 'You *do* know about him, don't you?'

'I know he's a nice kid.'

'Well, maybe we better fill you in,' Bill said, as if he hadn't heard. 'A few months ago we was worried about such a young lad out every night on his own so we decided we'd better have a word with Social Services. Thought it best.'

'You never know, do you?' Ida this time.

Ah but I do know. And I know you don't really care about his welfare. I've met your sort before. Right action, wrong reasons.

'I feel sorry for the lad. It's not his fault...what his mother does.'

'You're too soft.' Bill was quick to put her right. 'He's not the sharpest knife in the drawer. Right little nuisance. Appears on the dot of five and wanders up and down the beach like a stray cat. You can hear him muttering to himself. It's not safe, a boy like that, on his own. Anything could happen to him. I told him I'd report him if I saw him alone again.'

'Report him?' Too late to keep the harshness out of his voice. Abbott had fallen straight down the trap.

Walk on, Abbott told himself. *You don't need to listen to this. You don't need to get involved. They absolutely don't need to know a thing. Don't say another word.*

'Kids of that age should be at home at that time of day,' Ida said. 'But you see...we know what his mother does.' Her mouth set in a prim line. Her head nodded up and down like one of those toy dogs on the back shelves of cars. 'We know that men call at his house. Clients, like.' She stared at Abbott as if he were dim. Obviously the man didn't understand. 'His mother advertises herself as a masseuse but we all know what that means.' Ida waited for this earth-shattering news to stun her audience.

'I know.'

Two jaws dropped. Four eyes popped.

'Yeah, I know his circumstances and I know the boy. He's not at all stupid. Just a bit anxious sometimes. My friend who stayed in the red hut used to go for walks with him. She enjoyed his company.'

The need to protect the child from a different kind of predator won out over silence.

'Enjoyed his company,' Ida echoed, as if the words had no meaning. She stared at Abbott. 'But he's not very bright, as Bill said. We've been told he has trouble at school because he's slow and the other boys bully him. We think he should go to a special school.'

Oh fine. Shunt him off into a fenced pen and segregate him because he doesn't conform. Anyway it's rubbish. There's not much wrong with him.

'I don't agree.' He had to defend. 'He seems perfectly on the ball to me. Just doesn't knock around in a noisy gang. If it bothers you… him being alone… I can walk along the beach with him. While I'm here. I was thinking of doing that anyway.'

Yup, I already did and you know it, but we're all

playing games here.

It was their turn to be silent.

'Oh you shouldn't put yourself out. It's the mother's responsibility. Someone needs to put her straight,' Ida said. 'We heard the police were round a few months ago because the house was being used as a brothel. A petition went round the town to get it closed down. We signed it.'

I bet you did. Two women working together a brothel? And I bet you had a hand in its closure. So now she works without the protection of her friend. Congratulations. You made her life more dangerous.

'Someone should report him,' Bill said for the second time. 'I'm quite prepared to do that. We're only thinking of the boy's own welfare.'

Of course you are!

'I said I'm happy to spend an hour or two with him. He's a nice kid.' Abbott said firmly, and with a nod walked on. 'See you on the way back.'

Of course two voices continued in a loud whisper, carried on the wind. He couldn't catch what they said, nor did he want to. The damage was done and he was committed.

Committed? No, content. Because the thought of walking the sands each evening with the boy didn't worry him one bit. That first evening was like putting a tight, half-dead bud in water and watching it unfold and open. The boy's face had softened as he'd dropped his guard. Talking to him was not a chore. When the boy had left, he'd looked like an ordinary kid. Abbott had stood at his door and watched the boy walk along the beach and up the steps to the fish and chip stall. Then last night, bonded by a thorough soaking, his admiration had strengthened and he felt respect for a lad who had to tough it out alone, evening after evening, in all weathers, and who never complained. Respect and something softer. Maybe acknowledgement. Or even the stirrings of affection. He remembered how he'd put an arm round skinny shoulders and the boy had responded by folding in close. It had felt good.

You two don't know the half of it. You missed a whole new chapter last night, and if you did *know, you'd be reporting the pair of us to Social Services for indecent behaviour.*

The arrangement he'd promised was fine. It would be a punctuation mark at the end of the day before he poured the red wine and settled with a book in the glow of the oil lamp. Strange how quickly rituals became established, even in a bloody beach hut. In odd silences during the day, he caught himself looking forward to the boy's company. He liked the kid.

But for the child, Abbott's company would only be a stay of execution and that bothered him. Was it right to offer a hand of friendship and then withdraw it? He justified his decision with the hope that nothing would happen before the Vigilante closed up shop for the season or before the kid's solitary walks stopped for the winter.

Where did he go when it grew cold and wet? Surely he didn't sit in the bus shelter for an hour or more.

Abbott was aware that he was slowly letting down his guard. As each day came and went, the prospect of being followed to this small seaside town and led away to be charged seemed less likely. They weren't going to send precious resources after him for leaving his job. They might not even bother about the breach of security once the computer was checked. It was only the possible link with that single, insane past event that made him nervous. No-one knew he was here, and what he had done seemed a long way away, in time and place. Sharp edges had grown fuzzy, sometimes slipping from serious crime to a few big mistakes. One breach of high-level security. One love-befuddled slip into online adolescent but under-age porn. One runner.

No, Abbott. That's putting too innocent a slant on it. You accessed a site that is probably classified and almost certainly monitored and your name has been added to a growing group of men for whom only the most severe punishment is appropriate. You are on a list somewhere with serial pedophiles who are being hunted down in a cull that rightly has the law, the police, the media and ordinary citizens baying for blood.

Jim's voice broke in. *Come on, Abbott. Get real. You're not a celeb, mate. Not a politician. No-one bloody gives a damn about you. Hide away to your heart's content. No-one's interested.*

18
Day 7

I T WAS ONE of those end-of-summer afternoons when you could smell the residue of rain that had recently passed through and continued on its way. Clouds blew without purpose beneath a sky cleansed of colour. The sea's mood was restrained, its lapping subdued, the pebbles untroubled at the waterline. After the heavy rain, the weather was holding its breath.

The climate was in tune with Abbott's wish to take time out and give the hut a once over – a small, grateful offering in return for what it had given him. At the bottom of the steps he did a quick but thorough survey, looking for anything major that he might have overlooked in his brief comings and goings. At first glance it looked in good shape. The wooden stilts were fine – no cracks or splits or warping. The exterior paintwork had weathered well considering no-one had checked it for more than a year, but he penciled in next spring or summer for another coat or two. Yes, he would come back if he could. When he could. His aunt had used only the best materials, fastidious in her care of the place inside and out, making as many repairs as possible herself rather than entrusting them to other people, and he would follow in her footsteps. Fingering the paintwork around the windows and door as carefully as if checking a child for cuts and bruises after a tumble, Abbott felt for scars and damage and soft spots from the battering of wind and rain, but found only a few rough patches where the paint was starting to peel away. They would need sanding and filling but should hold up for another season or two. Round and round he walked, checking every plank and every join until he realised with a smile that he was also counting them.

Reassured, he turned his attention to the hut's underbelly, where a rotten plank or serious damp could undermine the whole structure. He squatted down, lay back and shuffled into the claustrophobic space, pushing himself along on his heels and elbows inch by inch across the rectangle of darkly shaded sand. He should have brought a torch because it was hard to see the surface above him even once his eyes had adjusted to the dark. With his hands, he scoured and searched the wood and found only minor signs of wear and tear. It needed only sandpaper and some TLC. Again he blessed his aunt for her care and surveillance.

Only once, while flat on his back, unable even to bend his knees, did the metaphor of his situation hit home.

Here he was physically trapped and ready for the taking. A sitting duck. If they were to come for him now, it would be all over; an ignominious exit shuffling out on his back to a ludicrous arrest.

With his head on one side, cheek pressed into the sand to give his neck a rest, he stared out at the beach, testing the image of the thick boots of armed police running towards the hut and discovering him underneath. Ridiculous. Or maybe they would assume he had left for a while and would stand waiting and waiting for his return. Could he hold out till dark, squirm out and crawl away?

Nah, that spy novel chapter was rubbish. There was no-one in sight. What was the probability of them arriving during the half hour he was spread-eagled under the hut? He sighed, shook off the image and scanned the beach, his eyes coming to rest on the dinghy which he'd so far ignored. Too engrossed in the small demands and delights of living inside, he'd not got round to checking it out, let alone putting out to sea in her. But the dinghy was partner to the hut, a legacy and a much loved vessel of childhood memories, all the more valuable for having been found, salvaged and restored. The boat had almost been lost to neglect, weather and time. Real memories pushed aside the imagined drama.

On their walks along the shore, he and his aunt had often stopped at a dinghy that had been pulled up towards the far end and which never left its parking space. Rumour told of an old fisherman who had reluctantly been taken from his cottage to a care home, perhaps leaving his boat as a reminder that once he had lived and fished here. Even before that, locals said that the boat had been taken out less and less as it became too heavy to be hauled in and out of the water and up the beach by thin, shaky arms. Fisherman and boat had both grown old.

After making discreet enquiries, his aunt had been granted permission by the local council to take it for her own use. Abbott remembered the day when, with the help of a couple of strong local lads, they had dragged it back to the small row of metal loops fixed deep in the sand at the end of the huts for boats which belonged to the owners. The pine oars were still in the brass rowlocks, maybe because, peeling and faded, they looked too clapped out to be worth nicking. He remembered proudly struggling back with one held upright in each hand, not caring that they banged hard against the sides of his knees.

She was a traditional thirteen-foot fishing dinghy, larch plank on an oak frame and copper fastened. A boat expert and experienced sailor who still harboured a secret wish to make one more trip across an ocean, his aunt had examined it minutely and meticulously, inside, outside and underneath.

'A couple of broken strakes so she's going nowhere until they're repaired. Or we can probably replace them and glue new planks in place with epoxy and secure them with copper rivets. Otherwise it's a matter of a lot of scraping and a lot of sanding and elbow grease. How strong are those arms of yours?'

'They'll be strong by the time we've finished.' He was eager to start, still ignorant of the punishing graft needed to restore the old vessel. 'Can't we scrape off all the paint and varnish her?' A ten-year-old Abbott hankered after a gleaning mahogany finish.

'Fraid not. There're layers and layers of paint, slapped on over a lifetime. It's ingrained. Stuck down cracks and holes. Even an industrial sander wouldn't get it smooth enough. Anyway varnish is for yachts and this is a working boat. It's traditional to finish them with lead paint.'

'What colour? Red?'

'No. White with a black line below the water.'

And so it was. She and Abbott started the repairs the next day by stripping out the rotten strakes but by the time his holiday was at its end, there were still weeks of work left.

'It'll give me something to do,' his aunt said cheerfully, her sleeves rolled up and a sand-paper covered block in her hand. 'Next time you come she'll be ready for the water.'

And so it was. On his next visit, on reaching the hut, he'd dumped his rucksack and run straight past, making a beeline for the pretty white boat tied with a thick painter and wire rope loop secured with a padlock in one of the metal rings sunk in the sand. In black paint, on her side, was the name *Magpie*.

The routine that holiday was to stay in the hut only on the wettest days and go for long walks or take out the boat on fine ones, though even on damp, windless days they would put on anoraks and wellies, climb into the dinghy and potter across a deserted, misty sea. Abbott let his hands trail through the water to make spurting bow waves. He and his aunt took turns rowing, his aunt still the stronger of the two, or they sat side by side holding an oar each, quickly establishing a strong, steady rhythm. Fishing didn't play a part in the excursions – he left that to the line-up of tourist boys on the sea wall with their rods and buckets who never caught anything – though he sometimes took a net just in case a tame flounder floated by. Mostly he fished out bands of seaweed coated in nature's slimy red bubble wrap, and feathers dropped from swooping birds.

They would row to the cove at the end of the beach when the tide was exactly right and no-one could get there on foot, pulling up the boat and claiming a stretch of beach that was all theirs. With pointy sticks, they drew circles in the virgin sand and wrote their names and played naughts and crosses. His sure-footed aunt clambered with him over slippery rocks and with slow fingers they carefully stirred rock pools where the sea life was not frightened off by a hundred noisy, prodding tourists.

And he remembered the never-exhausted excitement of racing wild into the cave and shouting his name and waiting for the echoes to bounce back, his voice like a noisy squash ball banging against the cave's sides.

On other days they dragged the dinghy down the beach and climbed in and pushed off, trousers rolled up, barefoot, simply to be one with the sea, out a few hundred yards, then a slow hundred-yard drift in comfortable silence, then back, the oars barely breaking the surface, cutting in and out as cleanly as sharp knives. The sea wouldn't feel them. They didn't hurt it.

Those memories still loitering, Abbott eased himself out and stretched tall to release the tension in his shoulder muscles. Then he patted himself down to bang off the clinging wet sand. These days he carried a grainy residue with him wherever he went. The boat called him. He was sorry he had neglected it.

It seemed to be in good nick but his key wouldn't move in the rusty lock, however deftly he tried to turn it, until he decided it wasn't worth the risk. If he kept at it, the key might break off. Back he trudged for some WD40 and a rag. That did the trick. Humming and immersed in his latest self-set goal, he dragged the boat down to the water's edge but not close enough for the waves to lap near it. Hunched over, seated on the central thwart, he ran his hands over the interior, feeling for damage and holes.

There was one small, rusty crack on the starboard side. Back at the hut again, he found his aunt's tool chest and carried it down, noting with a smile on opening the lid that all the tools were clean, oiled and sorted in sectioned plastic trays ready for any minor repair. A ghostly sun fell down a cloud-dimmed sky and began its journey to the horizon. It would be a bland and firework-free sunset.

It was while he was giving the repair a final rub with fine sandpaper, after filing the ragged edges of the crack and filling it with wood paste, that a voice floated across the bows.

'You've brought the boat down.'

He had lost track of time and forgotten all about the boy. It must be past five.

'I went to the hut first but you weren't there.'

'No. I'm here.'

'I saw you from the steps…what are you doing?'

'Been mending a small hole. She might be ship shape now.'

'Ship shape?'

'Fit for the water.'

'Wow. Are you going to take her out?'

'Maybe.'

The boy took a sharp breath in. 'Wow!' he said again. His eyes moved appreciatively over the neat shape, the white paint, the oars. Then he raised his face to the man where longing vied with hesitation. 'I've never been in a boat.'

'I know. You said.'

The boy looked at the man and the man looked at the boy. Neither spoke. The unspoken plea hovered between them while each breathed in and out and waited.

Say No. Say the boat's broken. Say you don't have life jackets. Say it's getting dark.

'I haven't taken her out yet. There may be other holes and leaks I've not spotted. I don't even know if she'll float.' *Excuses, excuses. They won't wash.*

'But she might. You said she was *ship shape.*'

'Well, as far as I can see on dry land.'

'I think she'll float.'

'Or she might fill with water and sink.'

'Not if you noticed the water coming in. Then you could row quickly back to the shore.'

'It might be a very slow leak.' He could almost hear the boy's mind racing to make the next convincing move. Like a game of chess.

'You could watch the bottom and see.'

'Yup. That was my plan.'

'Suppose… maybe I can sit on the bench?'

'It's called the thwart.'

'*Thwart.* I could sit on the thwart…that little seat at the front… and if she starts to sink I can jump out and we can pull her back.'

'The front of a boat is called the bow.'

'I like it there.'

'You told me you can't swim so you'd be no use dragging a heavy boat back through the waves. You might fall in. The water will be out of your depth and mine too in no time. Then what?'

He put his head on one side. 'Maybe you have life jackets?'

Clairvoyant or what?

Abbott didn't answer. There they stood side by side, staring at the boat and listening to the cross tide of wishes and vetoes that swirled in the space between them.

'There aren't any waves today. Sea's smooth,' Neville said at last.

The two stared at each other some more. Over the boat hung a great big helium balloon of hope and longing.

'S'pose she doesn't sink. S'pose there are no more holes...'

'Then that's fine. But I don't know that.'

'... and we can go out to the lonely green boat and have a look at her and say Hello. You can row, can't you?' His eyes darkened as he waited, stiff and tense, for an answer.

'Of course I can row. It's not me I'm worried about. It's you.'

Don't do it, Abbott. If you're seen, you'll be reported for absconding with an under-age boy. For endangering his life. You don't have permission to put this child in a boat and row out to sea with him.

He looked up the beach and saw that the

Neighbourhood Watch were planted on their verandah and weren't going away any time soon. They didn't even hide the fact that they were clocking his every move. On the table, he thought he saw a pair of binoculars. That should have settled it, but perversely it tightened his resolve in the opposite direction. Damn them. They weren't going to dictate his movements or interfere with his plans. What he did was fuck all to do with them.

'I've always wanted to go in a boat,' the boy repeated, his breath held and his shoulders hunched up high. Waiting for the blow.

Where's the harm? An eight-year-old boy who loves boats and the sea, but has never been afloat. I'll be gone in a day or two. This can be my parting gift. Something he'll remember. It's the least I can do before I dump the kid.

'OK. I'll take you out,' he heard himself reply and watched as the boy breathed out and jumped up and down with little skips of delight. Abbott saw his mouth stretch across his sweet face in the widest, toothiest grin. 'But at the first sign of the boat taking in water, we turn round and row the hell back. Yup?'

'Yup.'

'And on the water, I'm the skipper and you do exactly what I tell you.'

'Yup.'

'OK. First we go back to the hut and find the life jackets. You can have the one I used to wear when I was your age. My aunt kept it… maybe for a boy just like you.'

Neville stood very still for a minute, then ran round the boat to the man's side, wrapped his arms round his waist and buried his head in his filthy, sweaty, sand-encrusted t-shirt. Abbott stroked his curls and held him close. He didn't try to prise him off. It felt good to tune in to the intensity of the child's happiness and satisfaction.

Then the boy loosened his arms and pushed himself away, shouting, 'Let's go!' and he was off, up the beach at a run, his legs lifted absurdly high to get some traction on sand that had dried to a powdery density in the clean air of the cold front that had followed the downpour. The sky had cleared after the day's misty start, the grey giving way to a thin, watery blue. Light winds blew innocent puffs of cloud way out along the horizon. There was a safe on-shore breeze. An almost flat sea.

A perfect evening to introduce a boy to the wonders of pottering about in a boat.

19
Day 7

'RIGHT, CLIMB IN gently, don't rock her about, sit on the front thwart facing this way and hold very tight while I push her out.'

'OK.'

Quiet and obedient, despite the crazy pounding of his heart, a boy zipped into an orange life jacket and with wide, astonished eyes, moved with care and ease over the main thwart and took up his position in the prow. Small hands gripped the edges of the short thwart that rose high off dry ground.

'OK? Ready?' Abbott asked, as he coiled the painter, threw it into the hull and placed himself behind the keel ready to push. 'She may rock a bit from side to side. Just hold on tight.'

'OK.'

It took very little strength to push her to the edge of the water, and then she was afloat. No waves buffeted her and she made a smooth transition from sand to sea. Boat and boy barely moved while Abbott held on to the end of the rope, giving himself a few moments to check her over one last time. Satisfied, he waded out until the bottom of his shorts were wet and, lifting his long leg over the gunnels, he stepped in, trying not to tip her to either side. Steady, calm, he took up his position on the main thwart and seized the oars in a single graceful movement. The boat barely rocked. The boy didn't move a muscle. Only his eyes darted from man to boat to sea and back. There was no fear. No counting.

Beneath the water here there was no sudden cliff edge so the oars hit the sea bed for quite a long way out. The flatness extended well beyond the beach especially at low tide, as Abbott knew from watching holiday-makers wade out forever in the mud before finding water deep enough for a real paddle or swim. The change to a different depth was first felt in the movement of the boat as she lifted and surged forward. She was free.

'OK, you don't have to stay frozen,' Abbott said, turning round and smiling at the stiff little figure in the prow. 'But just don't make any sudden movements or we might sway wildly and you'll tip sideways. She's a light boat.'

The boy nodded, too awe-struck to speak. He loosened his grip a fraction and allowed himself to turn just his head and stare backwards to sea and sideways towards the cove. The man rowed on, pulling on the oars without effort so that the boat moved in a rhythmic pull and glide, pull and glide straight out into the bay. For a while, neither spoke. The wonder was enough.

It wasn't until they were about a hundred meters out and drawing level with the smaller fishing and sailing boats anchored nearest to the shore that the boy asked the question he'd clung to since they'd set off, not wanting to disturb the magic of the first moments.

'You said we could go to the green boat.'

Abbott turned his head. 'Yup. That's where we're heading next. I wanted you to get used to the boat first and to just enjoy the feel of her. Then you'll be relaxed on the water.'

'I'm already used to her. I love her.' It was heartfelt. Even passionate.

'Right, round we go. Green Boat, here we come.'

Weaving around anchor chains, then short stretches of dark blue emptiness, they slid on, both in thrall to the satisfying solitude of gliding over water while evening turned down the dimmer switches on sky and sea. Out here, the waves lapped softly against the hull and the breeze quickened, but it was eerily smooth. Like skimming over black glass. Night would not bring rain or wind.

'What's your name?' Neville asked, after acres of easy

silence. 'We're friends but I don't even know your name. That's funny, isn't it?'

'Abbott.' He was too relaxed and tuned to the boat to think of giving the boy his invented one. *He won't remember.*

'Is that your first or second name?'

'Both. Either.'

Neville put his head on one side, the cogs turning. He knew not to pry, not to intrude but he didn't understand this.

'Like Morse,' Abbott said, before realising it would mean nothing.

The boy frowned. 'Morse? I know about the morse code.'

'Don't worry about it. Morse is a TV cop who listens to difficult music and only has one name. Morse.'

Watched and loved by ageing Guardian readers. This isn't helping one bit.

'Does he solve the murders?'

'Always.'

'Is he very tough?'

'No, not really. He's gentle and clever but also determined to catch the baddies.'

'My mum doesn't watch that. She watches quiz shows and soaps like Hollyoaks. I don't watch anything much. I'd rather stay in my room and read.'

'Me too.'

'Abbott.' He repeated it quietly, then let it go. 'Abbott.

That's a nice name.'

'I know what a lie is. I mustn't tell lies.' It came out of the blue, after ten minutes of him watching the water spurt backwards through his fingers and watching the trail to see how long it lasted before fading back flat into the sea. 'But what if you keep quiet about something rather than telling? Is that a kind of lie?'

'I think it depends. There isn't one single answer to that question because the question is too big.'

'You mean sometimes it's OK and sometimes not OK?'

Where is this leading? Abbott thought he knew.

'Well… suppose I did something and I didn't tell my mum.'

Yup, spot on. Crime by omission. Lying by saying nothing. Quite a sophisticated concept for a boy of eight.

'It would depend if not knowing would make her angry or would upset her. Or cause her trouble. How about we stop talking in riddles and be honest and clear. This is about you not telling your mum that you spend time with me, isn't it?'

Neville sat upright on the prow, letting his hands drip puddles of salt water on to his lap. 'How do you know?'

'I guessed. Am I right?'

The boy nodded.

'You haven't told your mum about me, have you?'

'No.'

Abbott didn't jump in with an answer. After a while, he said, 'I guessed that too.'

''Cause it's… private,' the boy said. 'Something I do that no-one knows about.' He rocked backwards and forwards on the thwart, glancing up every few seconds, waiting to hear what the man would say.

What about the Vigilante? They know. But that's beside the point. This is about a boy trying to sort out right from wrong and about having a conscience. Tricky stuff.

'OK, this is what I think. You've known me only for a few days…'

'Six days.'

'…six days… and we've been for walks together and talked and eaten chips in my hut.'

No harm has come to you and soon I'll be gone. But that's not a good answer to your question.

'I know that but I've not told her. Usually I tell her everything.'

'Why haven't you told her about me?'

'In case she stops me seeing you.'

Exactly.

'OK, what would she say if you told her?'

'That I mustn't talk to strangers.'

'Do you know why?'

'Because on the TV there's tons of news about kids being hurt by strangers.'

'Am I a stranger?'

'Nope.'

'And most of those kids on the news were hurt in schools and care homes where they lived because they didn't have homes of their own.'

'Not on a beach.'

'No. Not on a beach. So I think you have to decide.'

'How?'

'It's very difficult but this is what I think… really and truly you should tell your mum.'

The boy stared over the gunnels into the blackness of coming night, disappointment and worry clouding his features.

'But that's a very simple answer and it's not a simple situation,' Abbott added. 'She's the one who sends you out by yourself every evening and so she's not there to supervise what you do. You met me and we became friends. In a way, she sets you free, doesn't she, and trusts you not to get into trouble.'

Abbott stopped rowing and twisted round to watch the boy's reaction. He, in turn, looked hard at Abbott. 'I understand when you explain things. I don't always.' He waited. 'So can I choose?'

'I think you can choose. And if you start to feel uncomfortable or uneasy about spending time with me then you should tell her.'

'I never feel uneasy with you.' Instant. Heartfelt.

'But if you do, I can come with you and we can both tell her if that makes it easier.'

'It might be.'

'Then shall we leave things as they are for now?'

Is that a fair response? Am I avoiding my responsibility because I enjoy the kid's company? And I feel he enjoys mine? Soon I'll be gone and he won't have this dilemma. His conscience won't trouble him. His mum will find out but it will be too late.

What with the slow row out to the green boat and now the boys' questions when Abbott had shipped the oars and turned to face him, letting dinghy drift, time had slipped past. For him too, the escape from the shore, from everything, had been a relaxing end to the day. He glanced at the boy's watch but couldn't see the face.

'Ten to six,' the boy said, following his eyes. 'I should be eating my chips now but it doesn't matter.' Nothing mattered. The pair of them had been lulled into timelessness by a boat whose slide across the water they could barely feel. Abbott took up the oars again.

'OK, as soon as we've had a good look at this boat, we'd better turn back.' He let the boat glide to a halt against the green stern and put out a hand to stop any damage and to catch hold of the taut anchor chain to hold them steady while they stared up.

'She's very pretty. I wouldn't mind a sail in her. Good shape. Good trim. Bet she sails close to wind.' He was talking to himself, caught up in his passion.

'Close to the wind?' The boy frowned. So much he didn't know.

'Yeah… lots of boats are like blunt bricks when it comes to sailing into wind so you end up tacking backwards and forwards. Very frustrating. A well designed boat can be steered quite close to the wind.' The boy looked bemused but listened keenly. 'A sailing boat relies on wind filling its sails, OK, so it's easy with the wind behind you or to one side. But if you need to go somewhere where the wind's blowing straight at you, then it's tricky, and some boats can get closer to the wind than others.'

It was all a bit hard. And there were too many new words. The boy tuned away, leant far out sideways to try to touch the boat himself.

'Careful. No, don't do it that way.' Abbott quickly saw the disaster scenario of boy in water.

'Can't reach.'

'I know. Wait. I'll pull up closer.'

With a stir of one oar they glided right alongside. Abbott's hand steadied the dinghy until she came to a rocking halt. The boy shifted on the seat, shuffled to the very end and leaned once more. With gentle strokes, he ran his hand up and down the hull.

'Been wanting to touch her,' he said with a shrug. 'I watch her every day.'

'I know. You said.' He understood this love of a boat. And a boy's fantasy.

'Sad no-one lives on her. She's all alone out here.'

'I know. It's a shame. She's a fine boat. I'd like to see her under sail.'

'Maybe you could buy her.'

Oh dear. Gliding across water does that to folk. Something about being adrift and cut off encourages wild thoughts.

'Then you could live in the red beach hut sometimes and sometimes in the green boat. You could go to different beaches and sleep in the cabin...'

And you're going to say you can come too.

'...and I could come with you. Sometimes. When you're not too busy.' The extra words were added like apologies. He'd heard himself pushing things too far. A glance back at the man told him he shouldn't have said those things.

'No, Neville,' Abbott sighed and gave him the reality check. 'The green boat belongs to someone else and maybe they'll come back soon to sail her again. She's not for sale. And I don't want a boat.'

'I know.' Subdued, the dream drifted away. 'I know that really.'

They sat in silence, Neville's hand still stroking the boat's hull as he gazed at her, misty-eyed.

'It's getting too dark to see,' he said, pulling himself back onto firmer ground. 'The green looks black now.'

'I know. We need to get back. Just a few more minutes.'

The evening was fast pulling down its shutters but even in the gloom he could see the boy's disappointment. Hard to tear the child away from something he had, until now, only dreamed of doing.

When Neville spoke again, his voice was very quiet, the words almost whispered. 'But I can wish… I can wish that you'll stay in the red beach hut and maybe buy a boat.'

'Yes, you can wish.'

But it won't happen.

'Wish you were my dad.' It was almost inaudible. Perhaps he thought his words would be carried away on the breeze and lost in the lapping of waves. His voice came from the folds of his anorak. His shoulders were hunched. Pretending to be invisible. He knew.

The first time it had been half serious. A wish thrown out in the joy of being in the red beach hut. This, the second time, it was the real thing and it frightened Abbott. He had watched the child lower his protective shield, bit by bit, as his trust grew with each new day. Each new walk. Each new conversation. Now he was exposing the soft centre of his being and it set off alarm bells and spinning red lights.

You have to stop this. Before he gets hurt. Before you hurt him.

Abbott let it go, pretending he hadn't heard. 'OK. Off we go,' he replied, his voice falsely upbeat, taking refuge in the practical business of readying the boat. His hands gripped the oars, dipping the paddles back into the water. With one strong shove he pushed the dinghy away from the green boat and let her float out into the bay.

'I don't want to go back.'

'I know.'

'Just a bit longer?'

'No. We're already late. You're late.'

'I don't mind being late.'

'But you're always punctual. Your mum will be worried.'

'I don't care. I'd rather stay with you.'

With a deep sigh, Abbott pulled on the oars and turned for the shore. It *was* late. They had stayed out far too long. The boy wouldn't get home on time. And Abbott had heard thoughts, previously guarded, that were way beyond what was real and right. A shell built from repeated disappointment was showing tears and holes through which Abbott saw a longing that would end in pain and hurt.

Jesus, Abbott, you do like getting yourself into trouble.

Back on the verandah of the white beach hut, two people had noticed and tracked the boy heading down towards the man and the boat.

'Now what?' Bill had got up to start stacking the chairs but stopped. 'That kid's back. Down by the sea this time.'

'Not going for a walk today then?' Ida was busy, tidying away plate and mugs. Folding blankets.

'No. The bloke's been messing about with that dinghy all afternoon. It looks like he's going for a row if I'm not mistaken.'

'So?'

'I'm wondering if he's going to take the boy with him.'

'Surely not.'

Ida finished what she was doing and went to stand at Bill's side. Both watched intently as the edge-of-sea activity unfolded. So little happened on this beach that they watched day after day, week after week. So little happened in their lives. This was high drama.

'He *is* taking the kid,' Bill said. 'Look, the bloke's been back to the hut for a life jacket and the boy's sitting in the boat. Well, I suppose we should be thankful for that. If he falls out, he might not drown.'

More staring.

'Look… they're on their way out. That bloke's a strong rower. The dinghy's fair moving through the water,' Ida said. Perhaps she too would have liked a ride.

'I don't care how strong he is, he's no business taking someone's kid out in a small boat like that. That boat's not been on the water for years. It could be rotten by now. It could spring a leak and sink.' His eyes brightened at the idea. 'That's not right, Ida.'

They followed the boat as it grew smaller and smaller on the flat sea. A child's cut out paper boat.

'They're way out now. Past the anchored boats,' Ida said, straining her eyes to see through the murkiness of the evening light.

'What does he think he's doing? It'll be dark soon.

He's taking a big risk, if you ask me.'

'Well, it looks like he can row,' Ida said, soothing Bill with a hand on his arm. 'They'll probably be fine. Nice treat for the boy.'

'But damn inconvenient for us. We'll have to hang on here in case something goes wrong. That kid might fall overboard. They might get into difficulties. We'll have to stay here in case we need to call out the life boat.'

Small sparks of excitement passed from one to the other.

'Well, I'll make another cuppa, shall I?' Not waiting for an answer, she turned to go back into the hut but Bill's next comment stopped her in her tracks.

'I took a dislike to that bloke the minute he walked past.' As if that were news. 'Rude, stuck-up bugger.'

'Didn't want to give us the time of day, did he?' Ida said appeasingly. 'But maybe he was thinking about that book he's writing.'

'Well he can act all superior but there could be something not quite right going on here and I have my suspicions.'

'What? I don't think the man's doing any real harm. He's stopped the kid bothering us. And he's kept the lad company on his walks, that's all.'

'No, that's not all. We've seen them go into his cabin a couple of times and they were still there after we'd packed up and were heading back. Seeing as what's in the papers at the moment, you just don't know, do you? I bet that kid's poor mother doesn't know what's going on.'

Has he forgotten that he'd been the one to tip off to the police about the two women working together from home? That he'd called the boy's home a brothel?

'You just don't know these days,' he repeated. 'I've asked people and no-one's seen him around here before. He's new to this town. We have no idea who he is.'

'I suppose not. Look, I'll make another coffee, shall I? They could be a while yet.'

Ida got away this time but when she came back with two mugs of Nescafé, Bill had moved their deck chairs to the railings so they had a front of stalls view. They drank and waited. Ida unfolded one of the blankets and wrapped it round her shoulders. The temperature was dropping and she hadn't expected to be here at dusk. Bill never felt the cold.

'Oh look… they're rowing back.' Ida stood up, thankful the vigil was nearly over.

'About time. It's nearly dark. Getting cold, too.'

They watched through the grey of an evening that turned people to shadows. They watched as the boat, a small blurry shape but still visible because of its white paint, slid slowly back towards the shore.

'They're back!' Ida announced, relief in her voice. Now they could go home. 'The bloke's jumped out and he's pulling the boat out of the water. I think I can see the boy at the front. Well, I'm glad they're safe.'

'Could have ended very differently.' Had Bill hoped

for that? Did this feel like an anti-climax?

Eyes screwed up, they watched as the taller figure leant forward and maybe held out his arm. The smaller one was standing up and making his way to the stern. Reaching for the steadying hand, he jumped clear and stood very still beside the man, beside the boat. The man had hold of the painter and was dragging the boat further up the sand. He made it look easy.

'Aaah!' Ida said, suddenly sentimental. 'They're having a bit of a hug down there, Bill. Look. Maybe the boy's cold.'

'Why's he hugging the boy?' Bill asked.

'Well, maybe like a father giving his son a hug after a nice time together.'

'But he's not his father. He's not even a relative.'

'He says he knows the boy. Says the woman who lived in the hut before used to spend time with him.'

'We only have his word for it.' Bill wasn't letting go.

The two figures on the shore blurred into one. The darkness closed around them.

'Oh that's all right, the boy's going on his way now,' Ida said. 'Look. He's turning his head and waving and waving. But he's sticking close to the shore and not coming up past us.'

'Wouldn't bloody dare.'

'It's a quarter to seven. It's dark. We'd better get on our way then.' At last.

'That boy shouldn't be walking home alone at this

time.' Bill ignored his wife's growing discomfort and her wish to go home and get warm.

They could see the boy more clearly now. He was running and taking the steps to the promenade three at a time.

'He looks happy,' Ida said.

'Happy or not, I think maybe it's time to pick up the phone and have a quiet word with the local police,' Bill said with a satisfied smile.

Ida frowned. *Now what?* 'I don't think there's any need for that, Bill. Let's pack up and go home. The boy's fine.'

'I'm not sure about that.' Bill said, warming to a subject that had been simmering for days. 'A strange bloke turns up out of the blue. Seems to live in a beach hut. Always with that boy who has nowhere to go of an evening. On the At Risk list, we've been told that, haven't we? They spend hours alone in a hut. Now he's taken him out into the bay in a small boat. Plus the hugging and kissing on the sand...'

'We couldn't see any kissing, Bill. They just had their arms round each other. Maybe saying Goodbye for the night.'

'Use your imagination, Ida. I think the police might be very interested. Just a friendly warning, like.'

'There's no need to make a fuss, Bill. Just leave it, will you?'

'No, I'm not leaving it. I don't want to be the one who

said nothing when we hear there's been trouble.'

Ida sighed. Her husband was bored and without a compass and had been ever since he'd retired. He didn't have nearly enough to keep him occupied. And she also knew there was no turning him around once he got a bee in his bonnet.

'They'll want a description and the bloke always has that cap pulled down.' Ida made one last feeble attempt to stop him.

'I got a good look in the light this afternoon through the binoculars when he was bare-headed and messing about with that boat. While you was tidying up. I can give a description.' A nod of self-congratulation.

'It may all be nothing. We don't want to waste people's time.'

'We can't take the risk. Not with what's going on nowadays. The world's become a dangerous place.'

Ida looked at her husband and knew his mind was made up. He was on one of his missions and she hoped the police would stop him very quickly in his tracks. She went into the hut to find another jumper.

'Stay there and sit still while I pull the boat up. Hold on tight.'

Neville didn't move a muscle. Only the expression on his face changed as sadness drifted across his neat features to push aside wonder and gratitude. He took the offered hand and stepped easily, proudly, on to the sand. He watched the man tug on the painter to pull the boat well clear of a further wetting and waited for him to stand still on the other side of the boat.

'You did very well. A sailor in the making.'

The boy beamed. He still felt the rhythm of the oars and the glide forward repeating like echoes through his body.

'But you'd better hurry home now. You're late. You'll be in trouble.'

Neither moved. Until the boy ran round to the other side of the boat and flung his arms round Abbot's waist and buried his head against his chest. Abbott accepted the boy's offering – awe and gratitude – and wrapped his arms round the skinny, trembling frame. He dropped his head onto the boy's tumbled curls and held him close.

'Oh… that was the best thing ever,' the boy said, his words muffled and buried in the man's t-shirt.

'Yup, it was good. Boats are good for the soul.' Abbott was lost for words as he tuned in to the undertow of this child's fierce and conflicting emotions.

'Come on. Time to go.' He un-peeled the clinging arms and gently separated himself.

The boy gazed up at him, still not wanting to break the bond. It was Abbott who cut free by picking up the painter and bracing himself to drag the boat further towards his hut.

So immersed was he in the relaxed ending to the gentle row out into the bay and back that he didn't notice the figure standing in the shadow of his hut until he straightened up ready to pull the boat further up the sand. Whoever it was had done a stealth job because Abbott had kept an eye on the shore. He must have crept along the beach close to the promenade wall. That was worrying. His heart flipped in fear. His hands shook so much he dropped the rope. *Now what?*

'Go home,' he said firmly to the boy while watching the person up on the shore. 'I'll see you tomorrow.'

'Yup.' The boy grinned and did his shoulder shrugging.

Wait. He wasn't thinking straight. 'Look, meet me by the promenade steps, not the hut tomorrow. OK? Can you remember that?'

'Why?'

'Because… I may have other plans. I can see someone up by my hut, so I may have a visitor for the night.' *Rubbish. Utter rubbish.* But he had to get rid of the boy.

God knows who's up there waiting for me and what it means. Or if I'll be there tomorrow. Whatever…The boy doesn't need to be seen hanging around the hut. He's not involved. My problem, not his. If he has to wait alone on the steps tomorrow, it'll look perfectly normal.

'OK. By the steps. Don't forget.'

'I won't.'

This time the boy did break free, setting off at a run, turning every few paces to wave. But Abbott's attention was elsewhere. With a thumping heart that had nothing to do with the exertion of dragging a boat up a beach, he set off up the sand.

20
Day 7

'JIM!'
'Abbott!'

'Christ, you had me worried there for a minute, mate. What are you doing here?' The high colour across Abbott's cheeks drained away. He was sweating and shivering. His heart in overdrive.

'Want a hand?'

Without waiting for an answer, Jim jogged to the boat and bent his back to push the stern while his friend pulled the painter taut and gave a long last tug. A smooth operation, just like always. The two of them had it stowed and padlocked in minutes.

'New little play-mate?'

'OK, leave the sarcasm 'til we get inside.'

Jim's helpfulness was short-lived. He shot his friend a furious look, his mood soured by the stupid slow journey.

And by having to turn up like a bloody child minder to sort out his grown up colleague. 'I've got a couple of hours to talk some sense into you and then I have to get back.'

'Fine. Shut up for a few more minutes and then I'll listen to your diatribe.'

'My sensible arguments.' Already he was mellowing, relieved to see his friend in such good shape after worrying himself sick that he'd find an emotional wreck of a hermit hiding in a hut.

'Come on in,' Abbott said, holding open the door and watching Jim's face as surprise and bemusement passed across his features. Obviously he had not expected this.

I bet he'd imagined me sleeping on the floor among deck chairs surrounding by bag lady plastic bags of pizza cartons and empty booze bottles.

'Nice place you've got here,' Jim said, inching his way round the confined space while Abbott got out two glasses, opened a bottle of red and pulled a packet of bread sticks from the cupboard. 'No, really,' he added when he got the raised eyebrows in reply. 'I'm not poking fun. I'm impressed. Really cosy pad. I mean if you've got to hole up somewhere, this is a good place to do it, mate. Nice one!'

'Well, thanks.'

'Not a problem. Praise where praise is due.'

'Look, there's only one chair so how about we sit on the floor with our backs against the bookcase?

The same as the night before. And the night before that.

'Fine by me. You're the big guy. If you can fold

yourself up, I'm sure I can,' he said with a smile, hunkering down, one hand holding on to the full glass. 'Cheers, mate!'

'Cheers, Jim. Thanks for coming, whatever you're going to say and however much I don't want to hear it.'

Two pairs of legs stretched out across the floor. Two hands raised glasses to lips. Two men crunched hungrily on bread sticks while the unsaid lay unwrapped between them.

'So what you been up to? Apart from taking kids out in your dinghy?'

'I'm not even answering that.'

'Who is he?'

'Jim, leave it.'

'OK. I'll presume it's above water, if you'll excuse the pun.'

'I said knock it off. None of your business. None of anyone's business what I do here.'

For a while they sat and stared and sipped, waiting for the vibes to regroup so that they could talk properly.

'Look, I know you've got your guard up but I've come to put you in the picture so I don't want any new surprises. You've given me enough to deal with. OK?'

'There's nothing nasty in the woodshed, if that's what you're thinking.' Still defensive. Still protective of himself. And the boy.

'I was thinking about something nasty in the beach hut.' It was only half a joke.

'For fuck's sake, Jim!' Abbott put down his glass. Placed a hand on the floor and bent his knees, ready to rise. To throw his friend out.

'OK, OK. Sorry. That was below the belt. I won't mention the boy again. Sit down and listen.' Jim placed a hand on the other man's broad shoulders to hold him.

Abbott sank. Sighed. Picked up his glass and downed a large swig. Stared at the floor.

'I'm listening,' he said. 'Though I don't like it so far.'

'I'm sorry. Started off on the wrong tack,' Jim said, pulling back a rueful smile at another awful pun. 'I'm a bit on edge. Out of my comfort zone.'

'Yeah.'

'I've come to tell you that things aren't as bad as you might think. To tell you where you stand. Here's the situation back at the ranch.'

The tension was palpable.

'Go on.'

'OK, your crimes. One, you didn't report the fact that someone hacked into your computer. I've talked to the chief and while he's none too pleased, he's not as angry as he was. Rap over the knuckles waiting for you.'

'That's all?'

'Yup. Scout's honour.'

'You said he was mad.'

'Initially… he calmed down.'

'And…'

'Two, they've traced the hacker…'

Abbott's head jerked up. He clenched his fists.

'Who?'

'An insider job. A bloke in IT who has a serious problem with gays. He covered his tracks pretty well… knew how to hide behind layers of encrypting but one of our lads was smarter than him. We've got him. He's been charged.'

The relief was palpable. For a moment the room swam. Abbott put his head down and waited for the dizziness to pass.

It wasn't Luke. It was nothing personal.

'Hate crime…' Jim was saying when Abbott tuned back in. 'People feel sorry for you. Can't be nice to be taunted.'

Abbott said nothing.

'OK, three. You scarpered. You walked away. That's a bit harder to excuse. You've got some explaining to do but not one single person I've told…'

'Who knows about it?'

'Your absence has kind of been noticed. And word gets round. The story on everyone's lips is that it was fucking bad luck that you were on the receiving end of someone's nasty prejudice. You were the victim.'

Abbott got up to fetch another bottle, uncorked it and refilled their glasses. He tore open a large bag of crisps and threw it down.

'Will I be charged for not reporting the hacking?'

'No. There's sympathy for you, mate. We know you

take flack for…'

'For being gay. Yeah. It happens.'

Abbott took a deep breath and let the air out long and slow. Like letting go of something that had been stuck in his throat for a week.

'I'll still be fired.'

'Doubt it. Not if you come back now. It's the running away that's upsetting folk. Looks really insane, especially as you have a reputation for being solid. It's the only thing you've done that seems dodgy.'

Again they sipped their wine, Jim giving his friend time to reflect. He knew not to rush him.

'Yeah. On reflection, it was bloody stupid. I panicked,' Abbott said, meeting Jim's eyes for the first time. 'I've impressed even myself with my idiocy.'

Jim smiled at the glimmer of humour. 'It was a bit of an odd move, mate. Out of character.'

But you've trodden very lightly over the other piece of the incriminating puzzle. This could have had a very different ending if the hacker had been someone I knew. Someone with a personal vendetta out to punish me. A long time ago I watched a beautiful young man use my credit card to buy porn. It could have come full circle.

'Is that it?'

'That's it.' Jim put an arm round the other man's shoulders, the same gesture with which Abbott had reassured the damp child.

'So what's the punishment?'

'Black mark on your CV and confined to a desk job for a few months. They know you love working with the lads and will hate watching the others lose a few to the nick where you might have got through.'

'Fair enough. You sure?'

'I'm very sure. I haven't rattled on a Noddy train all the way to this god-forsaken seaside town to bring you half-truths and lies. They want you back. They're worried about you, Abbott.'

'I thought they might come after me.'

'Got delusions of grandeur there. What you did is of little significance. *You* are of little significance. They just want you back in harness to save hiring some novice replacement. Sorry. Were you expecting Special Squad in balaclavas? They certainly aren't sending out the troops because one youth worker deserted his post.' Jim laughed. 'Look, your disappearance hasn't exactly made headlines.'

Abbott didn't dare confess that he'd been staring at The Mail expecting to see his name. Listening to Jim, it seemed to make sense. His crimes had grown into a grand opera with his imagination revving in overdrive.

'They want you back working with the lads. Soon. We don't have many with your experience or your skills. We've got a few new cases who need your touch once you've served time pushing paper around.'

'Did they send you?'

'I volunteered.' A tactful way of saying *Yes, they did.*

'I'll think about it.'

'No, you won't. You'll pack up now and come back with me. I've got...' he glanced at his watch. 'We've got one hour before the toy town train leaves.'

Mellow with wine and the company and support of his friend, and hugely relieved with the news that was several notches lower on the ladder of doom than he had anticipated, Abbott considered the offer. There really wasn't any reason why he shouldn't go back and face the music. Now rather than later. He'd had time to come to his senses. He could abort this insane flight from reality here and now. Jim was right.

'If you don't come back, it will be a different story,' Jim said, reading his mind.

'You mean no job?'

'Exactly.'

They sat a while longer, munching crisps, Jim knowing not to push any harder. His mate knew the score.

'OK.'

'You'll come back with me then?' Jim had reckoned on more of a battle.

'No. I'll come back tomorrow.'

'Why?'

'It will take me more than an hour to pack up here and leave the hut as my aunt would have wanted.' Only then did he beam in on the obvious question. The one he hadn't even asked. 'Is that how you found me?'

'Right first time. I remember when your aunt died. You hid your feelings like we all do but I knew you were upset. I remember you telling me she had a beach hut and you'd gone there when you were a kid. After that it was child's play. Your aunt never married so has the same name. I searched through the records of the deceased last year and found her, then found her address here. Phoned a few folk in the town council offices and was told about the beach hut. Not exactly rocket science.'

Of course Jim would have been able to follow the trail. Who were you kidding? You can't hide, you stupid sod!

'As I said, no-one's coming after you. You're not breaking any laws packing in your job or living in a beach hut that belongs to you, but it might get a bit claustrophobic in winter, and you might start to miss the work.' Jim threw his friend a piercing look. Ironic and mocking. So familiar.

'Thanks, Jim.'

'My pleasure. I miss you.'

The emotional atmosphere was ten degrees warmer. Ten degrees more relaxed. It almost felt like they were back in tandem working on a case together with a plaster board divider between their desks. Abbott felt a strong tug of nostalgia.

'So who's the kid?' Jim wasn't going to let it go. No loose ends.

'Just a lonely boy who walks on the beach every evening.'

'So you made friends with him?'

'Yeah.'

'Can't stay away from troubled lads, can you? Busman's holiday, is it?' Jim gave his friend a shove. 'Poor kid. He'll miss you when you vanish.'

Yeah, and that's the real reason I'm not coming back with you. Nothing to do with packing because I can come back and tidy up any time. I told the boy I'd see him tomorrow and I will. I won't break a promise. I have to say goodbye to him, not just walk away.

21
Day 7

S HARON WAITED AN extra twenty minutes for the client who hadn't turned up before swearing at the walls, kicking off her heels, peeling off her tight top and leggings and climbing into old jeans, a t-shirt and trainers.

Damn them. Why can't they phone me and tell me when they're not coming?

But they never do. Her time is of no interest or value. She threw the tarty bedding into the cupboard and returned her room to its everyday state. Six fifteen. Neville would be eating his chips on the wall. She peered out of the window and saw that the sky was clear and almost dark. Venus was up there for her nightly stint. She had time for one more glass of wine before maybe setting off to meet him. He'd like that. She celebrated the end of every work session with alcohol, just as she used it before the punters arrived to blur her thoughts and soften the hard edges of what she had to do. Most nights were two-bottle nights.

At six twenty-five, she slammed the door and stumbled down the first step. She put a hand on the bar to steady herself.

C'mon, Sharon. You've not had that much. Get your feet in line.

She expected to see her son at the end of the road, perhaps just turning the corner but he wasn't there yet. Five minutes too soon. And he'd been late a couple of times recently. Unlike him. She walked on, zig-zagging a bit and bumping into a few people who gave her filthy looks. She decided to head along the promenade rather than walk the beach because he would have climbed back up the concrete steps a while back. The promenade was in darkness, apart from the ugly lights of the stalls, but she'd recognise the outline of her son anywhere, and he wasn't there. Odd. Continuing on her way, she stopped at the chip stall where the bloke poked out his head ready to greet a new customer and take a new order.

'Have you seen my son?' Sharon asked.

The man knew exactly who she meant, but decided to take the opportunity to express his disapproval that the child was left wandering alone every night and dredged up at his stall in all weathers for a cone of chips. Nice kid. Shame about the mother.

'Who's that then?'

Sharon sighed, understanding the game that was being played. Lots of people played games like that with her. And she agreed. From the outside looking in, it didn't look good.

'Neville. You know perfectly well. He buys chips from you every bloody night.'

'Oh him! The little boy who walks along the beach all by himself for hours…'

'An hour or so and not every evening.'

'Oh, that's all right then, isn't it?' If words were stones they would have hurt her.

Sharon blew out another angry breath which told the stall holder just what she'd been pouring down her throat. 'Look, stop messing with me and just tell me if you've seen him tonight?'

'Hard to remember sometimes.'

'Stop playing fucking games.'

'And you start taking care of your son.'

'I do.' Through gritted teeth. She wasn't giving him any more.

'Oh yeah? So it's OK that the poor little bugger sits on the wall over there and eats chips after wandering about all evening…'

'I just said. For an hour or so.'

The man leant his elbows on the ledge where kids reached up for their chips. 'If you open your bleary eyes, darlin', and look down over there, you might manage to see that your son is standing on the beach. He's not come for his chips tonight. Must have had something better to do.'

Sharon looked down. The man was right. The view swam and blurred.

'What's he been doing then?'

'Don't ask me, darlin'.'

It was hard to see so far away and the lights on the promenade had just come on, glowing pale before they warmed to yellow, making the beach behind almost invisible. Leaning over the wall, she squinted through the darkness. Outlines and shadows. Dark figures against a dark sea. She blinked away double vision.

'Is that him? Standing by a boat?'

The man stuck out his head and made a deliberate show of straining to see. 'Yeah... I'd say that was a boat. I'd say that might be a boy standing next to it.'

Sharon ignored the sarcasm. 'And there's a bloke down there with him, isn't there? He's with a bloke.'

'Could be.'

'Who?'

'How the hell should I know? He's your son, not mine.'

He's with the big man with the kind, open face who always buys the boy the biggest cone of chips. Seems to be looking out for the kid. Taking care of him. Never seen anything but kindness there. I'm not ratting on him to you. He's the one who keeps the lad company of an evening.

'He didn't take Neville out in that boat, did he?'

'Not a clue. Been serving customers all afternoon.'

Like hell you have.

Sharon was still staring at the shore. Hard to make out what was happening in the failing light, but she thought she saw the smaller figure go round the boat and fuse with the bigger one. For a while they didn't move.

'Look, just tell me. What's been going on down there? Neville's not been in the boat, has he?'

'No idea.'

'Please.' Sharon's eyes spilled tears as she looked up at him and silently pleaded for the truth.

'I saw the boat go out. Didn't see if your lad was in it.' The lie was deliberate and taunting.

'He didn't take my son out into the bay, did he?' she asked, incredulous. 'He can't swim. He might have fallen in.' Sharon gasped.

'Couldn't tell you. Maybe he did. Maybe he didn't. As I said I was busy serving customers. S'pose he did? Didn't you know he was off on a little boat trip…not that I'm saying he was.'

'Of course I bloody didn't know.' Panic took over. 'I'm going to call the police. Do you know the man?'

'No.' His tone changed to serious. 'Look, love, isn't it your job to find out who your little lad spends his time with?'

'Will you at least back me up then? Look where I'm looking now. You can see the two of them together.'

'Too dark to see a thing over there and me, I don't like

talking to the fuzz. My story is I seen nothing. Sorry, you're on your own.'

'Jesus! If he's hurt a hair on my son's head…' Sharon's voice was high-pitched and hysterical, the alcohol swimming in her bloodstream.

'And what's the police going to do? Your boy's already on the At Risk register.'

Sharon's mouth fell open. 'How do you know?'

'Come off it, darlin'. Everyone knows. You tell the police he's been hanging about with a man you don't know and he'll be taken into care.'

He was right. It was true. She had no power. She was on her own.

'Might be better for the lad if he was.' The chip man threw his final poison dart.

'You bastard.'

She turned away and made a half-hearted attempt at a run to meet Neville, a small black shadow who was now on his way across the sand towards the promenade steps. Through the fuzziness, her son's recent words reverberated, telling her about the client who had frightened him. *Bloody hell!* But that was ages ago and this is now and there's no connection. *Come on, Sharon. Pull yourself together. This is probably nothing to get upset about,* she told herself, as the alcohol smoothed her anxiety and she searched for easier scenarios to deal with. Perhaps she'd over-reacted. He'd tell her. He was close enough now for her to see that he had a broad smile on his face.

'Mum!' *What's she doing here? And she looks upset.* The smile froze on his lips as he climbed the stairs two at a time and walked hesitantly towards her.

'Son, where have you been? I've been worried.' Her anger and upset spent on the chip man, she felt deflated and weary. Had she made a fuss about nothing?

'Same as always. On the beach.'

'But you didn't go for your chips and it's a quarter to seven.'

'Fifteen minutes late. Sorry.' He looked up to see if he'd get a row.

'It's OK. As long as you're all right. Come on, let's walk back.' She didn't feel like another encounter with the stall holder. She could make him microwave chips. 'You can tell me all about it and what you've been doing when we get home.'

'Nothing much to tell.' The first lie.

'Well… I was a bit worried when you were late.'

'Is that why you came to meet me?' *Does she know?*

'Not really. The last man didn't show up and I had time on my hands. Thought I'd come and find you on the wall but you weren't there.'

Neville breathed more easily. Maybe she'd seen nothing and his secret was safe. 'I was just watching a man take his boat out and the time went quickly.' Saying it like that was a risk. The second lie. He waited.

'It's OK, son.'

Like the chip man said, whose fault is it that the boy's out there on his own?

'How about we have chips together tonight? Got some in the freezer.'

'Yup.' It was going to be all right. Neville gave a small skip of relief at his mum's side.

'So you was watching a man take out his dinghy?' Sharon had stuck the packets of chips in the microwave and was dumping them out onto two plates. She took the tomato sauce from the cupboard. 'Sorry. We've run out of vinegar. You've got the salt?'

'Yup.' Neville was making a show of shaking it on his chips. They were limp and tasteless, not like the crispy ones in the cones with the mouth-tingling vinegar.

'You know him, son?'

'Nope. Just a man.' His third lie.

'So what were you doing down there instead of sitting on the wall?' Her words were still a bit slurred. She was bone tired and longing to get Neville to bed so she could curl up on the sofa and watch some mindless TV. And perhaps open another bottle. The alcohol in her veins made the domestic scene slightly out of focus and her previous anxiety and anger faded into a numb acceptance and resignation. Like every night. Some mornings she woke on the sofa, still dressed and with the TV on.

'So you never met this man before?' Just enough

energy for a last push at what her son had been up to. If anything.

'Nope. He walks along the beach sometimes and waves. Tonight he dragged his boat down to the water and went out in it.'

'And you stood and watched?' Something didn't ring quite true. 'Why? It must have been nearly dark. You couldn't have seen much.'

'I could hear the swish of the oars for a long time. I could just about see the boat 'cause it's white and I wanted to make sure it came back safely.'

'Since when have you been interested in boats?'

Neville looked up and saw his mum's tiredness. 'I'm not really. It was just something to do.' The fourth lie.

'You're not counting your chips,' she said, registering a silence, even though he didn't always count out loud. 'You aren't counting.' It was like part of their conversation was missing.

I am. I'm counting lies.

22
Day 8

'I SHOULD HAVE phoned last night. When they got back from that dinghy ride.' Bill was standing to attention on the verandah of the hut, scanning the beach and watching the red hut as the sky once again dimmed and darkened. He'd been on edge and on the lookout for the man all day, hoping to catch him and give him a few home truths. Maybe it would all have ended there, anger dissipated. But waiting in vain had made him irritable. He half-anticipated more drama but under the adrenalin there were niggling doubts that he was barking up the wrong tree. He smothered his reservations. He'd started down this track and had to see it through.

'Well no, Bill. Last night ended with no harm done,' Ida said, trying to smooth things. 'We saw the boy meet his mum up by the chip stand, didn't we?'

'I'm not waiting tonight if I see them. Enough is

enough.'

'Well… it depends what they're doing, surely? If they go out in the boat again then maybe you're right and it's time to tell someone.'

Both searched the beach for two figures. They watched and waited.

Bill's loud shout made Ida jump. 'Ah! There they are. Look. On the promenade steps tonight. They're not starting at the hut. Why's that then? They always start at the hut.'

'That's a change, isn't it? But they're off down to the beach now, holding hands. Yes, they're off on their walk. Same as always. Back into the hut afterwards.'

'OK, that's it. I'm going to phone the police.' But still he didn't. Perhaps he knew that he had nothing to tell them. Nothing they'd take seriously.

'I don't think there's any need, Bill.' Ida said. But she wasn't holding the phone.

'That's for the police to decide.' Bill was finally dialing the number of the local police station which he knew by heart from phoning to complain about noisy or drunken youths on the beach. And tramps. Or parties. Or about anything else he didn't like. They knew him. Bill was both a useful informer and a bloody nuisance.

'Yes. Good Evening. It's Mr. Sinclair here. I live on the estate in Brown Hills. Bill Sinclair. I'm sorry to bother you but I'm a bit concerned about what's been going on down here on the beach and I thought it best to give you a call. I'm worried about a boy who's on the At Risk register who's been with a man we don't know…'

'I'll just put you through to the front office, Sir. Hold on, please.'

'Thank you.'

Silence.

'Yes?' A woman's voice. Very calm. 'You're worried about a child on the At Risk register I believe, Sir? Is that right?'

'Yes. He's been spending a lot of time with…'

'We don't deal with that, Sir. If the child's on the register and you're concerned, you need to dial 999.'

'999?' Bill was put out. 'Isn't that for emergencies? This isn't exactly an emergency…'

'You need to dial 999, Sir. This is classed as an emergency.'

'So you won't be dealing with it yourselves?'

'No. Not if the child is on the register.'

'I thought I could have a talk to you first. Maybe come down to the station and put you in the picture and you could tell me if there's any need to worry A bit of a chat like…'

'No. You need the emergency services, Sir.'

'Oh. OK. Thank you.' Bill clicked off and stood there puzzled. And put out. The doubts danced in the pit of his stomach.

'Well, Ida,' he said, 'apparently I have to dial 999 if the

kid's on the register. I hope I'm doing the right thing. I don't want them saying I'm making a fuss about nothing. I thought they'd just want a few more details, you know, so they could maybe send someone down and check themselves.'

'It doesn't seem right to be dialing 999,' Ida replied, touching his shoulder. 'But now you've reported it, I suppose you have to do what they say. You can't leave it there.'

Bill hesitated, but seeing the man with his arm round the boy's shoulders, heading for the cove, he picked up his mobile again and dialled. But not eagerly. Not with any enthusiasm.

'999. Which service?'

'Um...police please.'

'Thank you. I'm connecting you to the police now.'

The next exchange from operator to emergency services was rapid and allowed Bill no time to change his mind. Or even to string together his story.

'Police.'

'Yes, good evening. I want to report a man who picks up a young kid on the beach every evening. The boy's on the At Risk register. Am I through to the...er...right people? You see, I just phoned the local station and they said to phone you.' Bill expected to be re-directed. It must be a mistake.

'If the boy's on the At Risk register, you need to talk to us first, Sir.'

'Oh. I see.'

'We'll need to ask a few questions.'

'Fire away.' Bill was relieved he hadn't made a fool of himself.

'First, are you sure this man isn't the child's father?'

'Absolutely sure. The man's a complete stranger. Only been here the past week and he's living in one of the huts, not just coming down for the day like the rest of us…'

'And you say he picks the boy up each evening?'

'Yes. They spend an hour or two together.'

'How long has this been going on?'

'Living in the hut or spending time?'

'Spending time with the boy.'

'It's been six days now.'

'So what's worrying you, Sir?'

'Well… the boy always goes for a walk along the beach at five o-clock while his mum works as a…er…masseuse. He walks to the rocks by the cove and back, then buys chips and eats them on the sea wall or in the bus shelter if it's raining. Regular as clockwork. Then I suppose he goes home.'

'So what exactly do you want to report?' The voice was brisk.

'That's all changed since this man turned up. The lad spends every evening with him. They go for walks until they're out of sight and they seem very close, if you know what I mean. They hold hands and sometimes the man has his arm round the boy. We're a bit concerned things may not be…er…quite right.'

'How old do you think the child is?'

'Oh, he's seven or maybe eight.'

'Where are you calling from?'

'We own the white beach hut. I'm there now. A few doors away from the red one where the man's living. My wife, Ida, and I come down every day so we've been watching. We're both worried about the man picking up this little boy and taking him back to his hut.'

'Where are they now, Sir?'

'They're heading for the cove at the end of the beach. But perhaps I should just add that they've spent a couple of evenings together in the man's hut with the curtains and blinds closed. The other night it was raining cats and dogs and the boy was soaked to the skin after their walk and took off all his wet clothes before going in with the man… we think we saw the man wrap him in a towel.'

'I see. Anything else that you've seen that might be relevant?'

'Yes, last night the man rowed the boy out into the bay in a small dinghy, the boy sitting in the front. They were gone for about an hour and a half. They got back in the dark but safely, thank goodness, but that was the final straw…'

'Thank you.'

'I hope I'm not troubling you for nothing. I mean it's only what we've seen. The wife and I. I hope I'm doing the right thing reporting it. It's just with the boy already at risk…'

'There's a police car in the vicinity. I've sent out a call so if you can stay where you are please.'

'Oh.' Not what he had expected. 'Right.'

'Wait where you are please. Officers are on their way now.'

'We'll be here.'

'They'll be with you soon to take a statement. And they will decide if any further action is appropriate.'

'I see.'

'Can you tell me how long ago they left your sight?'

'About ten minutes ago.'

'Can you tell me what the man was wearing?'

'Yes. Jeans, trainers and a big thick coat. And a dark cap.'

'And the child?'

'He always wears the same. Khaki shorts and a green anorak and jelly sandals.'

'OK, I am updating the officers with the information you have given me so far. Can you tell me anything else about the man?'

'He's white and looks a professional type. Well spoken. We've exchanged a few words. Not a tramp or anything like that.'

'His height?'

'Quite tall. Probably about six foot.'

'And his build? Can you describe him?'

'He's well built and fit looking. Strong.'

'Can you still see them now?'

'No, I can't. They've gone too far along the beach and the light's fading.'

'Did the child seem distressed in any way?'

'No. But he's an odd kid. Not the sharpest knife in the drawer if you know what I mean…'

'Has he ever seemed distressed?'

'No. He behaves like he likes the man. He's on the At Risk register.'

'Yes, we have that information, Sir.'

'Oh… a police car has just turned up on the promenade. There's two police in uniforms getting out…'

'Right. Good. I'm going to hang up now so you can speak directly to the officers and they'll decide on any follow up action.'

'Yes, they're making their way down to the huts…'

'Well, I'll leave you in their good hands. Goodbye.'

'Goodbye.'

'Bill, there are two policemen walking down the steps and coming this way,' Ida said, pulling hard on his sleeve.

'I know. I have to tell them everything…what I've already said on the phone. They'll decide what to do next.' Despite the cool chill in the air, Bill's forehead was beaded with sweat. This wasn't quite what he had imagined. He thought it would be a quiet chat over digestive biscuits and a handshake for being an observant, cautious citizen. Then maybe a police or Social Services visit to the boy's mum. This all seemed a bit out of proportion.

'It's not like I reported a terrorist attack,' he ventured, sounding nervous and unsure. 'I hope I've done the right thing, Ida.'

Ida was too busy staring at the approaching men in uniform to reply.

'They look very serious, Bill. The way they're walking…and they're in uniform.'

'We can handle that, Ida.' *Couldn't they?*

'Maybe they'll want to catch the two of them together because it's only my word.' Bill felt a sudden need for justification and a terrible sickening fear that this might all rebound on him. 'And with all the news of men messing with boys. Better safe than sorry.' It was a question. He wanted an answer.

'That'll be it. Then it's up to them, isn't it?' Ida had gone pale under her tan.

'Yeah. They'll know what to do.' Bill sounded like he'd had the stuffing knocked out of him.

'Well, we'll just tell them what we saw. I'm sure it will be fine,' Ida said.

Seeing Jim had been like being given a hard push through an escape hatch back into the real world. As the week had worn on, he'd barely looked in that direction, moving instead in mind-numbed, well-heeled tracks from the hut to the beach, from the hut to the shops, from the hut to the cove. Then back. How thoroughly, even contentedly, he'd played the game, shrinking his life into small routines carried out against the elemental movements of the tide and the soothing encroachment of the water working its pebble-dashed way up the beach to the seaweed line on the shore, then pooling back to the sea. The monotony of the soundtrack was the perfect backcloth for someone who wanted to blank out the recent past and its consequences. Life in the hut had been sufficient, even necessary, but then Jim had come and interrupted the withdrawal with true words about a real life, a life which included Abbott, even if he'd convinced himself otherwise.

After Jim had left, he'd refilled his glass and sat without moving, replaying the conversation, beginning to make the first fine emotional adjustments towards leaving his sanctuary. The physical packing up was nothing. It would take him a couple of hours tomorrow to fling his things in his bags and leave the place ship-shape. His emotions, complex and noisy, might take all night to knock into a shape that he could parcel up and take with him when he walked out of the door. Jim had brought other voices with him which now occupied the previously silent space. They talked on. About his duty and his work which was his calling. Of his foolishness, and the idiot act of running away. They called to him and made themselves heard across the comforting sounds of the sea and the wind until each word was as clear as writing and required an answer in action. After more emotional squirming, tethered still to a place which required nothing from him and which gave him an illusion of peace, he accepted Jim's clear incisive call to return to the unfinished business of a life he had screwed up. But not irreversibly.

Abbott got to his feet, unsteady after the third bottle, and heaved himself up on to the bunk. It would be his last night here. This time. Maybe forever. Lying with his arms folded under his head, he blocked out the sounds of the English beach and made a firm decision that he would leave straight after he'd been for his last walk with the boy the following evening. He would not renege on that. His bags would be ready. He'd say a gentle farewell back at the promenade steps, a place which held no emotional ties, rather than outside or in the hut where the memories he shared with the boy were too precious and too sharp. After their walk, he'd give the boy a brief plausible explanation, say goodbye, send him on his way. Then he'd come back here to collect his bags and head for the station. Parting from Neville would be the hardest act in a sequence that would see him back on home territory by the morning.

23
Days later

Dear Neville,

I hope this letter reaches you very fast. I stuck on a 1st class stamp which means you should get it in 1-2 days instead of 3-4 days but I bet you noticed and know that already. I'm writing to tell you I am very very sorry for what happened on the beach on our last night together. It was frightening and upsetting for you and I regret that very much.

The police held me for a long time and asked me lots of questions about what I did in the beach hut and on the beach during the week I was there. They asked me about being friends with you and what we did together and what we talked about. I only told them what they needed to know, not our private conversations. I know the police came to your house and asked you lots of questions too. I want to thank you from the bottom of my heart for being brave and honest because your answers meant that in the end, the police let me go. Our stories were consistent. A bit like *constant*. The same. Remember that word?

Guess who caused all the trouble? It was the couple in the white hut. Yup! You were right about them. The man phoned the local police after he'd seen me taking you out in the dinghy and he told them it was a very dangerous thing to do. And he told them that we went for walks together and your mum didn't know, which was true. So the police turned up thinking there was trouble and that maybe I was a bad person. That man made everything we did sound much more scary than it really was. He should have told your mum first, not the police, and then we could have sorted everything out without that last horrible, scary night on the beach.

I imagine that you are feeling very hurt. But however badly it ended, I want you to know that I enjoyed being with you on our walks and in the hut eating chips together. I enjoyed our conversations. You're a great kid, Neville, and I want you to believe that.

Right now, I am back at my desk with a lot of paperwork and some bad boys to see. I didn't talk to you about my work but that's what I do here. I try to stop boys from getting into more trouble when they've been caught by the police nicking stuff and getting into fights and hurting people. Some of them go to prison. Some of them try to be good. I've been doing this work for a long time and I like it.

I got a big row from my boss for taking a break in the beach hut without telling anyone at work. That's why I turned up out of the blue. Sometimes a person just needs to escape. I bet you can understand that.

I don't know when, but I will come back. I'll write to you and tell you when I'm coming so that you can start walking past the red beach hut and staring at the window to see if there's a warm red light inside. Next time, I want to meet your mum and explain what happened. I'll ask her if we can go for walks together. I can even collect you from your house. Then everything can be the same as last time but without nosy people watching us on our walks and telling tales. You know, don't you, that I would never hurt you?

If you want to write to me sometimes, I would like that. It doesn't matter if you don't. I think of you as the clock on my wall at work shows 5 o'clock and imagine you walking down the steps from the promenade and setting off on your walk along the beach to the cove. Soon you will have to swap your jelly shoes for wellies, and the sun will be sinking faster and lower in the sky. Will you have to stay at home then?

When I come back, we can go for walks in the dark sometimes if your mum agrees and we can count the stars in Orion. Would you like that?

I miss you.

Your friend,
Abbott

About the Author

Lynn writes, has always written, and runs Linen Press, the only independent women's press in the UK. It's a fine balancing act but ever since she watched Elvira Madigan, she's secretly wanted to be a tight rope walker.

Her fourteen books are published by HarperCollins, Longman, and The Women's Press.

When not writing or editing, you'll find her building a house and creating a landscape out of rocks in an oak clearing high above a small village in southern France. Hands on.

Find the author via her website:
lynnmichellauthor.co.uk

More From This Author

Run Alice Run

Alice Green realises that being over fifty is much the same as being invisible, so why not make the most of it? Her head-in-the-sand husband doesn't notice the mountain of clothes and the piles of stationery.

When two police cars draw up outside her house in leafy, upmarket Edinburgh, Alice back-tracks through her memories, recasting the events – and people – who chipped away at her confidence and contentment over the years. What happened between the heady university days and the sad marriage to a husband who gets more excitement from his computer than from his wife?

Run, Alice, Run is an irreverent coming-of-middle-age novel which looks with irony at the way society defines and diminishes women of all ages.

Praise for Lynn's Previous Works

Run, Alice, Run. IQ Press, 2014. Linen Press, 2018.

'Run Alice Run traces the breaking points of a young girl's heart and the ways in which each fracture moulds her into the woman she's become at the novel's start and end.

– Isabelle Coy-Dibley, The Contemporary Small Press

'In this eloquent novel, Lynn Michell ultimately weaves a poignant tale of hard-won freedom.'

– Jenny Garrod, Dundee University Review of the Arts

'A very rare thing – a literary novel about female ageing and sexuality that pulls no punches, and it should be applauded for that.'

– Chapter and Verse

'With a voice as unique as its heroine, Lynn Michell tells the story of one woman's attempt to understand and acknowledge her past in order to secure and save her future. Her characters are strong and believable. Her settings in Birmingham and Edinburgh are recognisable and fresh, yet coloured by the emotional baggage that Alice brings to them.'

– Brook Cottage Books

'Melodrama interlocks with irony and subtly paints a portrait of the ageing beautiful woman in Western society. Alice feels she becomes invisible. Her husband is married to his computer. And instead of breaking that computer over his head, she starts stealing and stealing becomes a habit….The strength of the book is its humour and that humour remains, despite the drama and the serious issues posed in the narrative about women in today's society.'

– Laura Martignon. Amazon reader.

'Engrossing and believable. It even made me understand better my own time of acting oddly. I wanted to keep reading until the end.'

– Odaline. Amazon reader.

Shooting Stars are the Flying Fish of the Night. Linen Press. 2013.

'In this book, I recognise many of the mistakes I myself have made. If you dream or plan to sail off into the blue, you will learn from this book. A great read for those who are going or want to go over the horizon!'

– Sir Chay Blyth

'*Shooting Stars are the Flying Fish of the Night* should be compulsory reading for anyone intending to make their first extended offshore trip under sail. It is an endearing human story of three members of a family; father, mother and son battling to survive both physically and emotionally. Few families put thermselves through such a test and then have the courage to commit it all nakedly to paper.'

– Chris Hawes, Yacht Fractions

White Lies. Linen Press. 2010.
Runner-Up in the Robert Louis Stevenson Award

'A debut novel which possesses and is possessed by a rare authority of voice… It is the mother's voice that sings White Lies into unforgettability. Hers and Eve's. Their thoughts and writing ring like music.'

– Tom Adair, *The Scotsman*

'Hauntingly beautiful… with a bombshell of an ending.'

– Michele Hanson, *The Guardian*

'Moving, memorable and totally absorbing. Captures perfectly the trials of a middle-aged woman trying to care for and build a relationship with her distant father, now in his dotage, through the writing down of his memories.'

— Sophie Radice, *Guardian* & *Observer* columnist

'Credible and touching. Dramatic and tragic.'

– The Torch

'An anatomist of the human heart.'

– Wanda Whitely, HarperCollins

'A first class read. Transports the reader whilst exploring the reactions, feelings and fears of those who lived through the early stages of the Emergency.'

– Martyn Day, Lawyer for former Mau Mau insurgents against the British Government

'A wonderful evocation of Africa…Lynn Michell is an extremely accomplished writer. There are passages of extraordinary vividness and beauty and the characters spoke to me very convincingly. I love the sense, by the daughter, of unease at her father's painting of a golden era of colonialism, the spaces, the gaps that he is unwilling or unable to discuss.'

– Edwin Hawkes, Makepeace Towle

'A naturally gifted writer and not afraid of ambitious projects as this one is. It has great filmic potential.'

– Christopher Rush, author of Will

Readers' Reviews from Amazon

'This book is beautiful and well constructed. There are moments of playfulness and moments of love in the abandoned houses of Lake Navaisha. For the rest, the tenor is dramatic: beauty and war and human pain. This book that has shaken me.'

– Martignon

Beautifully written and page-turning. The story is told in David's, Mary's and their daughter Eve's voices, and in places you get three versions of the same events. Everyone re-writing history, telling white lies, to suit themselves. I loved this book – picked it up two days ago and could not put it down.

– A Reader

The child Eve's vivid evocations of a life of great, if temporary freedom in her African garden and surrounding landscape are viscerally painted. I feel her younger sister Clara's hot skin under Eve's fingertips as they strip off their outer clothes and draw letters on each other's backs...Weeks after reading this book I am still thinking about the characters and their story.

– Tracemyself

Shattered: Life With ME. HarperCollins. 2003.

'A timely and powerfully written book and Lynn Michell is uniquely qualified to write it.'

– Bernard MavLaverty, author of *Cal, Lamb, Grace Notes, The Anatomy School, Midwinter Break.*

'Inspiring stories, not simply of broken lives, but of survival and hope in the face of terrible adversity.'

– Dr Vance Spence, Chairman of MERGE

'Throughout this book, the reader is kept on a steady and reassuring journey of validation and support. The stories by other ME patients work to solidify Michell's broad but well-rounded overview of a life made more difficult by an invisible chronic illness. Identifying with the ME stories in this book reminds us that we are not alone in this fight.'

– CF Alliance Newsletter 2003

'Shattered is a powerfully written account of life with ME — an unpredictable and devastating illness. Definitely a 'There but for the grace of God go I' book, and one that should throw some much-needed light on this terrible condition.'

– *Tuam Herald*, June 2003

'I highly recommend it to all who suffer from ME/CFS...Shattered is a good eye-opener for carers, friends and relatives of sufferers who may not understand what it's really like to live with such a debilitating illness.'

– Sleepydust.net

Letters To My Semi-Detached Son: A Mother's Story. The Women's Press. 1993.

'A story of such painful intensity that tears poured down my face as I read it. No mother could fail to identify with her anguish and guilt, or her sense of failure.'

– Celia Dodd, *The Independent*

'A very modern situation that will send a sympathetic shiver down any parent's spine.'

– Hazel Leslie, *Mail on Sunday*

'A brutally honest account of how her own emotional needs and those of her little boy came into conflict. The sheer despair and desperate sense of guilt is something most mothers could identify with.'

– Jean Donald, *The Herald*

'Moving, tersely written and painful to read. The honesty is remarkable. I was left with some uneasy feelings, like I had read someone's diary, but then, perhaps, the controversial nature of this book is its strength.'

– Penelope Aspinall, Event

Growing Up in Smoke. Pluto Press. 1990

'If you want your children to grow up healthy rather than kippered in tobacco soke, this is the book you need.'

– Claire Raynor

'Essential reading for evey adult who smokes.'

– Lynn Faulds Wood

Lightning Source UK Ltd.
Milton Keynes UK
UKHW02f2009220618
324666UK00005B/8/P